With firelight playing off the red in her hair, the ivory of her skin, Boyd was lost.

Knowing he must move carefully, he touched the back of her hand with one forefinger. When she didn't shake it off, he stroked in tiny circles. He kept his focus on her hand, turned the palm upward, and continued the circles.

"There's something between us. You know it. I know it. From that first day, I wanted to lock the classroom door, toss you onto the desk, and make love to you. I know you feel something, Paula. Your hand is trembling as I touch you."

Where he touched her palm, the skin felt scalded. Honey flowed through her veins, thick and heavy; she became lightheaded. He dipped his head to replace fingers with lips. His hot tongue traced tiny circles in the center of her palm. As a ragged cry escaped, she grasped his hair with her other hand.

He slid his arms around her waist, and his mouth found her throat. He lifted her sweater to rub his face against the bare skin of her belly. The stubble of his beard excited every nerve ending until tiny fires burned everywhere.

Boyd heard her cry and rejoiced. He raised his head to see her face and found everything he needed to know.

She wanted him.

Praise for *AUTUMN DESIRE*

"*AUTUMN DESIRE*—a perfect 10—has depth and two characters with great chemistry...when it explodes, it is hot. Ms. Noble's dialogue felt real, and her writing style is clean and crisp."
~Romance Reviews Today

"*AUTUMN DESIRE* is an emotionally complex and vibrantly hued romance...a delightfully unconventional romance that proves middle age isn't middle (or end) of the road when it comes to falling in love or taking risky chances with one's heart."
~Cheryl Jeffries, Heartstrings Reviews

"*AUTUMN DESIRE*—a deep character study— Sharon Noble provides her audience with a strong look at a woman seeking self-actualization."
~Harriet Klausner, Amazon.com

"*AUTUMN DESIRE*—This is the kind of book you'll read over and over, like watching your favorite movie. Boyd Mackenzie...he's charismatic and wise as well as a romantic and inventive lover, and despite her misgivings, Paula finds him irresistible. Get a cup of coffee and a comfy chair."
~Susan Sinclair, Amazon.com

Autumn Desire

by

Sharon Noble

Autumn Desire

Cover Art by *Rae Monet*

The Wild Rose Press
PO Box 708
Adams Basin, NY 14410-0708
Visit us at www.thewildrosepress.com

Publishing History:
Previously published by Five Star Expressions, 2006
Last Rose of Summer Edition, 2010
Print ISBN 1-60154-760-9

Published in the United States of America

Dedication

To Brendan, who brought me roses.

CHAPTER ONE

"Good morning, class, and welcome to Biochemistry two-oh-one. I'm Professor Mackenzie."

Paula Wincott looked up with a start. Boyd Mackenzie, fair-haired boy of the Chemistry Department, stellar draw for graduate students all over the world, teaching sophomore level chemistry? Had the University of Colorado suffered such serious financial losses that high-ranking professors were reduced to teaching introductory level courses?

"Some of you may be wondering what happened to Professor Sloan, who was listed in the course catalog as the teacher for this course," he explained in a deep, supple voice while writing the course name and number on the dry erase board in a big bold scrawl. "Maybe you signed up for this section because he was scheduled to teach it."

He turned back to the podium. "Every now and again the Dean of Arts and Sciences and the Dean of the Graduate School get together to rotate some of the Profs from upper-level courses to freshman and sophomore courses to keep us in touch with the student body as a whole."

A silky female voice behind Paula sighed. "He can keep in touch with my student body anytime. The whole or any part he wants, any time at all."

"Mine, too." A giggle echoed beside the first girl. "Isn't he the most gorgeous thing you ever saw? Ooooh, just looking at him makes my nipples tingle."

"And the best part is he's single," the first one gushed. "Mmmmmm, I think I'm going to need a lot of extra attention this semester."

1

"Me, too. Do you think he teaches help sessions?"

"Help, help," the first voice murmured, sending both girls into soft titters.

Paula blushed, embarrassed at what the two had said, and afraid someone might think the words had come from her. She couldn't help noticing that Boyd Mackenzie was indeed gorgeous, although she couldn't imagine what that had to do with anything academic. Mentally she chastised the coeds for their lack of serious attention to their schoolwork. In her day society would have considered the forward behavior of this generation cheap, but, as her daughter Emma so often reminded her, times change. She would simply have to get used to it if she was going to be a college student again.

College student. The words sounded odd after she had spent so many years as a wife and mother. Now, suddenly, she was back in the classroom, in Biochemistry 201, where she had left her education behind so many years ago.

Professor Mackenzie smiled. "This semester it's my turn to introduce you to Biochemistry two-oh-one, and, if you're still here in the spring..." He waited for his remark to sink in.

A ripple of subdued laughter ran through the classroom as students glanced around to guess who might fail in the first semester.

The professor acknowledged the humor, then continued, "I'm also teaching a morning section of two-oh-two. You may continue with me or choose another section when the time comes. If you need to see me outside of class time, my office hours are posted at the Chemistry Department Office."

He wrote his name, big as life, and office number on the white board, then reached for the class roll and began calling names. Paula studied him covertly, this upstart who had charmed the entire chemistry department, this fellowship-snagging scholar who had so boldly moved in and deprived her husband of his rightful and well-deserved position in the department.

Sam had never introduced her to Boyd Mackenzie, and she had always had a mental image very different from the tall, broad-shouldered figure who stood before the class, exuding boyish charm despite his distinct middle age. She already knew he was a lot younger than Sam, but she wasn't prepared for the virile good looks. The Devil certainly had power to appear pleasing.

But she knew him for what he was. Sam made that perfectly clear.

"Wincott. Is Paula Wincott here?"

Paula realized she hadn't been listening. How many times had he called her name while she was assessing his physical appearance? "Yes. I mean, present," she stammered.

She ducked her head and tried to scrunch down in her seat, hoping she hadn't made a spectacle of herself. She had embarrassed herself already, and this was only the first five minutes of the first day of class.

Fortunately, the class was large enough so that no one paid any attention. The professor continued calling names, cheerfully unaware of her discomfort. Glancing around, she observed the disproportionate number of female students, although he also appeared to be popular with the males. Obviously his good looks matched his reputation as a teacher, an observation made with irritation. She didn't want him to be popular or a good teacher. She wanted him to be a failure. After what he had done to Sam, he deserved to be a crashing failure.

Then he was at her desk, handing her a printed list of textbooks and lab periods. She reached out to take the paper, refusing to look up and meet his eyes. His hand almost touched hers. She noted the long, lean fingers, the back of the hand sprinkled with fine, dark hair and tanned to a toasty beige. Then he was gone, moved on to the next student. She choked on the surge of anger flooding her chest while everyone around her carried on, totally unaware of her emotional state

That made her all the more angry. She wanted everyone to detest him as much as she.

Mackenzie returned to the lectern and looked around the classroom, relaxed and completely charming. "I'm happy to see we have an unusually large class this semester. Welcome to everyone. I encourage you to ask questions and bring any problems to me. I realize that not everyone is working at the same degree of understanding, which is why I'm here."

He said something about tutorials for those who might need extra help, but Paula tuned him out. All she could think of was the indignity Sam had suffered at the hands of this smiling charmer who was oblivious to her enmity. She kept her eyes lowered. Surely if he looked into them she would skewer him with the sheer force of her hostility, and she wasn't ready for a confrontation—not yet.

The remainder of the class passed in a blur. Her mind raced while she tried to think of an escape route from a suddenly intolerable situation. She could not, would not, sit in this man's class a minute longer than was absolutely necessary. When the students laughed at one of his jokes, she was reminded again of the personal charm he had used to such success in his move against Sam.

Thankfully, the bell rang, signaling the end of the period. The other students bolted for the door while Paula gathered her notebook and handbag. Because the professor had positioned himself at the door, she had no choice but to acknowledge him as she left. But she would not be caught so easily. She hunched her shoulders, dipped her head, and tried to slip past him. Just as she reached the door, he took a step forward. "Excuse me, Miss. You're Paula Wincott?"

He offered his hand, which she pointedly ignored and still refused to meet his eyes. She was close enough to smell the clean aroma of soap and water, and it disgusted her. He waited a moment, then dropped his hand and continued in a genial tone.

"I get a fair number of mature students from time to time but never one named Wincott. Are you by any chance Sam Wincott's daughter?"

Sam's daughter indeed! Her husband had been eighteen years her senior, so she'd heard the same assumption a hundred times. It still offended her. Unable to contain a burst of temper, she jerked her head up. "Certainly not! And you might as well know I hold you responsible for what I am—Sam Wincott's *widow*!"

Clutching her books tightly against her chest, she strode from the classroom and out into the bright Boulder sunlight.

****

Back in the classroom, Boyd replayed the last few minutes. She couldn't be Sam Wincott's widow. Sam had been close to seventy years old when he died, and this woman was still in vibrant middle age. He had never met Sam's wife, but the male faculty members had often spoken of the beautiful younger woman he kept to himself. Now, here she was, in Boyd's class.

What did she mean—she held him responsible for her widowhood? Sam Wincott had died of a heart attack. It had been a sad shock for everyone, including Boyd, but the man had pushed himself as hard as he had pushed his lab students, and his health had finally failed. Why did his widow's anger fall on Boyd's shoulders? He shook his head, hoping he had somehow misunderstood her. That had to be the answer. A simple misunderstanding.

CHAPTER TWO

Paula fairly flew from the Chemistry Building to the Arts and Sciences Building, an old, majestic structure that spoke of maturity and stability. The aroma of polished wood in the hallways emitted a comforting sense that all was right with the world. She marched straight to the Dean's office and took her place in the Drop/Add line, determined to drop Mackenzie's 201 section and add someone else's section—anyone else's section—as long as she didn't have to see and interact with this man three times a week for the next sixteen intolerable weeks.

While waiting for the line to whittle down, she considered dropping out altogether. Why would any middle-aged woman go back to college after all this time? Even when she was young, except for a special connection with chemistry, she'd never been a particularly zealous student. What had possessed her to consider returning to the classroom after being a contented wife and mother for thirty-two years?

Then, she remembered the telephone call that had changed her life.

"Happy birthday, dear Nana, happy birthday to you," sang the two off-key voices in something resembling, but not quite arriving at, harmony.

There was nothing new in the birthday message on her answering machine. Her two grandchildren sang to her on every birthday. Usually she loved to hear their sweet little voices wishing her a happy day.

Except... this was the day she turned fifty.

And she was alone.

It was her first birthday without Sam. She faced a long road of birthdays to come, knowing he would never be there again. She had been alone for a year, and would always be alone.

Pain burrowed in to find all the secret recesses where she tried to hide from the reality of her husband's death and the emptiness that followed. At first, friends rallied around, offering emotional support, doing what they could to ease his passing. But as time went on, she knew they expected her to pick up the pieces and continue with her life.

What life? She had no life without Sam. He had been husband, father, lover, teacher, and protector throughout her entire adult life.

A naive, inexperienced eighteen when she sat in the Biochemistry 101, she'd been captivated by his maturity, his dark good looks, and his passion for his subject. She had been surprised and honored when he showed an interest in her, pursued her, and quickly married her. At thirty-six, he was at the height of a brilliant career, strikingly handsome, and the object of the adoration of his female students.

Exactly like Boyd Mackenzie. The irony was not lost on her.

Her parents were dismayed when she announced her intention to marry Sam, considering him far too old for her. Plus, they had wanted her to finish college and have a career before she married and settled down with children. But they were soon won over by his charm, and the wedding took place with all the trimmings in her parents' home. She had pushed any potential problems to the back of her mind in the glow of newlywed bliss. Sam had been her knight in shining armor, her Prince Charming, everything she ever hoped for in a man. He was perfect.

Before she knew it Paula was pregnant with

Morgan. Emma arrived two years later. Sam was content with this arrangement. And so was she.

It was exciting to be Sam Wincott's wife and the mother of his children. He was highly respected in his field, a hard-working scientist whose research opened windows in the arena of plastics and resins. He was always in demand for seminars and consultation all over the world. Proud of his accomplishments, proud to be Mrs. Wincott, and proud to be the mother of two perfect children, thoughts of returning to school retreated to the back of her mind.

"Help you?" a bored clerk asked when Paula found herself at the front of the line. "Drop or add?"

"Both." Relief surged as she pushed her class enrollment card across the counter. "I'd like to drop Biochemistry two-oh-one, section one, and add section two of the same course."

She would soon be out of Boyd Mackenzie's class and, if she was lucky, she would never see him again in her lifetime.

The clerk adjusted a pair of thick glasses, ran a pudgy finger down the course list, then looked up without expression. "You can drop section one, but section two is already full."

"Already? Classes only started today. Check again, would you?"

The dough-faced girl shrugged her shoulders and looked at the list again. "It's full." This time she didn't bother to look up. "And there's a waiting list. A *long* waiting list."

"All right," Paula said, fighting rising panic, "All right, I'll drop section one and add section three. Section three can't be full already."

Section three met on Tuesdays and Thursday and ran an hour and a half, but she was willing to take the longer class. She would do anything to avoid Mackenzie and his snake-charmer cordiality.

The clerk rolled her wad of gum from one cheek to the other before perusing the list again. "Sorry. That section has been canceled."

"It can't be canceled." Her voice sounded shrill even to her own ears. "Why is it canceled?"

Students in line behind Paula began to shuffle their feet. She heard mumbling from the rear but would not be deterred. "Look, help me a little here, okay? My advisor tells me I have to take Biochemistry two-oh-one, but I *have* to change sections. That's all I want to do, just change sections. Maybe someone in section two would like to swap with me." She gazed hopefully at the clerk. "Could you check? Maybe ask someone?" She gave the clerk an earnest stare. "Someone might be dropping section two."

"Sorry," came the listless reply. "All we do here is drop classes and add classes. Do you want to drop Biochem two-oh-one or not?"

Grasping at straws, Paula clutched the counter and tried yet again; hysteria put an edge in her voice. "I—I have special circumstances."

Brilliance struck. "Hardship! That's it, hardship. I can't make it to class on Monday, Wednesday, and Friday. Can't you bend the rules a little? I have family responsibilities."

Running out of options, she was desperate. "Please."

The clerk stopped chewing, looked Paula firmly in the eye, and spoke slowly and clearly, as if to a child. "Ma'am, you're holding up the line. You can't add section two. Do you still want to drop section one?"

The system and this unflappable clerk had defeated her. "All right, yes. I'll drop it."

The clerk stamped the enrollment card and pushed a receipt across the counter. Though Paula's mind spun, she managed to retrieve the receipt and fumble her way to the door. Outside the Arts and Sciences Building, she sat on a long wooden bench to gather herself together. She watched students go by, students younger than her own children. Young, bright adolescents who had the world by the tail.

Would she be able to keep up with them? She hadn't been in school in so many years. If she failed, what would Emma and Morgan think of her? What would Sam have thought? What would she think of herself?

When Paula finally told Emma she planned to enroll at the university, Emma reacted with dismay. "Mom, have you lost your mind? Why on earth would you want to go back to school after all this time?"

Emma braided four-year-old Chloe's hair into pigtails while Paula tied bright blue ribbons on the ends and the child sang one of her endless, unintelligible nursery rhymes.

Paula reacted characteristically. "Oh, I don't know, honey. You may be right; maybe I'm too old. Maybe I can't learn as fast as I used to." She reached for another strand of Chloe's thick strawberry blonde hair. "I thought it might be a way to stimulate my brain and occupy my time. You know I've been at loose ends since we lost your dad. I thought it might give me some focus, a sense of purpose."

Emma's dark eyes, a legacy from her father, held puzzlement. "But you don't need to stimulate your brain. For what? It's not as if you're going to get a job at your age."

"I'm not looking for a job."

"Dad left you financially secure, and your family occupies your time."

"That's true. But the days are long, and I can't spend all of my time with you and Wesley and the kids. I'd like to get out and meet people."

"Mom, you have two grandchildren, and if Morgan would stop womanizing and find himself a wife, you would soon have more. That would be a perfect way to occupy your time." Finished with Chloe's hair, she turned the child toward Paula. "Everyone says she looks just like you. Here, give Nana a big kiss."

Her daughter obviously considered the discussion over, and Paula didn't want to cause friction by prolonging it. She gave Chloe a hug and received a juicy kiss from rosebud lips. She was devoted to her grandchildren, but lately she had begun to have a vague feeling there might be more to life than children and grandchildren.

She wasn't exactly sure what it was, but it continued to niggle at the back of her brain like a song that won't go away.

CHAPTER THREE

Sitting on the bench outside the Dean's office, Paula considered her predicament. If she wanted to get an education at the University of Colorado, she had to attend class. To do that, she'd have to enroll in Biochemistry 201. But not this semester.

If she was lucky, she could stall until Boyd Mackenzie no longer taught the lower level course. With that, she put the receipt in her handbag and, in a black mood, walked across campus and up the hill to where she had parked her car.

Boulder was at its most beautiful on this glorious autumn afternoon. Cotton-ball clouds played across a rich blue sky while gold and red leaves crackled under her feet. The crisp, clean air carried the unique scents of fall. It was her favorite time of the year. And Sam's.

The beginning of a new school year had always been exciting for him, though the three years prior to his death had been deeply depressing. Having fought vigorously against forced retirement, he turned into an angry, bitter man and took his disappointment out on her because he'd been unable to avenge himself on his rival, Boyd Mackenzie.

Mackenzie had enjoyed a fine reputation long before he was recruited to CU, having made a name for himself at McGill University in Montreal as a brilliant biochemist with an unbeatable knack for securing government grants and private donations. Though his area of study was disease control, he was a strong ecologist even before it became fashionable.

When the Chemistry Chair, Ed King, suggested

making him an offer, the faculty, including Sam, was enthusiastic. Though Boyd and Sam seldom saw each other except for staff meetings, they were congenial when their paths crossed. Sam was in inorganic chemistry, Boyd in biochemistry, so their work never brought them together. Then, ever so gradually, inexplicably...

"Hello again."

Paula was brought back to the present with a start. Standing just feet from her, Boyd Mackenzie was about to get into his car. It suited him, the metallic grey sports car with burgundy leather seats. No family for him, it was obvious. Imagine being as old as he was and still running around in a sports car. Clearly he considered himself quite the man about town. One more reason coeds flocked to him. Revolting.

Her instinct was to ignore him, but he wouldn't allow it. He quickly closed the door to his car and caught up with her just as she reached her own well-worn station wagon. "Paula!"

She turned brusquely, searing him with an acid tone. "It's Mrs. Wincott to you, Professor."

He nodded, but pressed closer. "Of course. I'm sorry. Mrs. Wincott, we need to talk. I can't accept what you said to me earlier. May I buy you a cup of coffee?" He gestured toward the coffee shop at the end of the block.

"No."

She opened her car door, but he persisted. "I'm sure we've never met, yet we appear to have a misunderstanding. Help me sort it out."

Ignoring the entreaty in his eyes, she fumbled for her keys.

"I said no."

"Please. I won't take much of your time, and we need to clear the air if you're going to continue in my class."

"I just dropped your class, so we have nothing to discuss," she snapped. "And I have nothing more to say to you. Step aside."

"You've accused me of some responsibility in your husband's death. That's inaccurate and unfair, and I don't accept it. You owe me an explanation for blowing up at me in my classroom."

"I owe you nothing but my profound contempt."

This man was not one to give up. He took her elbow in a gentle hand, and said, "If we could sit down together and talk, I'm sure we can clear this up."

His argument made sense, even to her. But she didn't want to sit across a table from him, look into his clean-cut good looks, and talk. Loyalty to Sam wouldn't permit it. She had to hate him, as her husband had.

Stomach churning, she jerked free of his hand and backed away. "I said no!"

She shook her head vigorously and rubbed her elbow, as if to remove his touch. Not only was she angered by his persistence, she was confused. "You must know my husband despised you. How can you think I'd want to spend a single minute with you if I didn't have to? Now please, leave me alone."

As their gazes held, she saw questions in his eyes, but she gave nothing back except a hard-edged stare. At last, he stepped back, palms raised in a gesture of surrender. Then he dropped his arms to his sides and shook his head slowly.

"I didn't know your husband despised me. And I'm very sorry to hear it. I don't know what's going on, but I won't pressure you." He took a step back and waited as she quickly opened her car door and slid into the driver's seat. "If you change your mind, you know where to find me."

He stood leaning against the car next to hers as she started the ignition and put her car into gear.

"Please think about it," he called as she roared away.
****

The day couldn't have gone worse and she still felt unnerved after she arrived home. It was as if everything had conspired to ruin her attempt at re-entering the world. She took off her shoes and placed them neatly in the shoe bag inside the closet. She folded her sweater and put it in a drawer, then hung the grey skirt on a hanger.

A place for everything and everything in its place. That's what Sam had always said. Simple domestic routines helped restore normalcy to her routine, and her emotions. She was just contemplating a long hot shower when the telephone rang.

"Hi, Mom," Emma rattled quickly, "Where have you been? Did you get my message?"

Paula sat on the edge of the bed and ran her fingers through her hair. "I just got in and haven't played the message machine yet." She made an effort to sound chipper, but it was an effort, and she didn't want to continue. "I was just going to have a shower and lie down for a little while. Tell the kids I'll call them later."

"Aren't you coming over for dinner?" Emma pressed. "Chloe and I spent the afternoon baking a cherry pie, and Wesley's bringing home ice cream. I have a roast in the oven, and we're looking forward to seeing you."

She'd forgotten about the dinner invitation. There was no way out, and in truth, it might not be a good idea for her to be alone tonight. Isolating herself was only an open invitation for self pity.

"I'll be over about seven. See you then."

She replaced the receiver in its cradle and sat back on the king-sized bed she had shared with Sam. She lay back on the pillow and stretched out her arm to his side of the bed, as if to touch him. It was flat, cold, and empty. Tears welled, then gave way as huge sobs racked her body.

She wept not so much for his death but for his youth. He had been such a warm, vital, talented man, a devoted husband and father, and a credit to the university. The years had slipped by so quickly, so effortlessly, while she wasn't looking. And when she looked again, her beautiful young husband had become an angry old man, irritable and demanding. She had loved the man she had married and who she knew still lived inside, but her words and deeds often went unheeded, her love unappreciated.

After she had cried herself out, nothing had changed. She was still there on the bed, still alone, and still not doing anything with the rest of her life. She sat up to unhook her bra. A shower was a start.

It was a few minutes after seven when she rang the bell on her daughter's front door, actually looking forward to an evening with her family.

"Hi, Nana!" Six year-old Ben opened the door and yelled, "Mom, Nana's here!"

Before she could respond, he scampered back into the living room where the television was going full blast, monster robots crushing entire cities as the inhabitants ran screaming for cover. He jumped onto the end of the sofa and aimed his toy ray gun at the television, shouting bloody threats at the top of his lungs.

"We're in here, Mom," Emma called from the kitchen, "Come on back."

Paula found her daughter bent over the open oven, basting potatoes and carrots with the juice of the enormous chunk of beef that shared the roasting pan. Seated on a high stool at the kitchen counter, Chloe sang *Old MacDonald Had a Farm* with a mouthful of raw carrot. Paula scooped her up and hugged her, then twirled her around a few times before depositing her back on her stool.

"Cawwot," the little one offered, holding out a half-eaten vegetable. "Bite, Nana."

Paula obligingly bit off a piece, then turned her attention to Emma, who had closed the oven door and turned her attention to wiping Chloe's mess from the counter.

"So, how was your first day in class?" she opened, fixing her mother with a penetrating glance as she wiped her hands on a dishcloth.

Because an admission of disappointment would give her daughter an opening to castigate her again for wanting to pursue an education, Paula shifted slightly and replied with forced earnestness, "Fine. Yes, fine. I think I'm really going to enjoy getting back into learning. I didn't realize what I've missed all these years."

She covered the lie by opening a drawer and reaching for place mats and napkins. Emma pushed on. "So, what courses are you taking? Surely you're not planning a degree program."

When Paula didn't respond, Emma asked, "Mom?"

"I really hadn't thought that far ahead, but yes, I thought I might finish my B.A.," she acknowledged reluctantly. "Of course, there's no rush. My faculty advisor recommended I finish up the rest of my sophomore required courses, then we'll talk about declaring a major—if I decide to continue. You know, one step at a time." Hoping to discourage further inquiry, she took out plates and silverware. "Okay if I set the table?"

"You're behaving as if you're a young student with a future ahead of you, like a job, a career. You don't have to take a degree program at your age. Why not just take a few courses that interest you?

"Unh huh," Paula responded absently.

"If you don't have enough to fill your day, you could take music appreciation or art history, or maybe a watercolor course in the fine arts department."

She paused for a moment. When Paula didn't reply, she continued brightly, "You could even take folk dancing over in the Phys Ed department. Lots of older folks take it as a non-credit course."

The *older folks* reference stung, but Paula let it pass. "Well now, that certainly sounds interesting. Maybe I'll take some of those courses." Hoping to avoid further confrontation, she moved onto new terrain while preparing to set the table. "How is Wesley enjoying the new office?"

"I love it!" Her son-in-law bounded into the room, large carton of ice cream in hand. "I have a corner office with a huge window. On a clear day I can see all the way to Denver."

He gave Paula a warm hug and kissed her soundly on the cheek. "How's my favorite mother-in-law?"

It was his habitual opening, and she loved him for it. She loved him for many reasons, this tall, lanky fellow who had charmed her daughter with his easy personality and quirky wit. His sandy hair was perpetually rumpled, and his brown eyes sparkled behind tortoise-shell glasses, but he was extremely attractive, and Emma was crazy for him. She positively glowed whenever he entered the room.

"She had her first class today," Emma answered, lifting the roast from the oven and settling it onto a large platter. "Ask her how it went."

She turned back to the stove while Wesley steered Paula into the dining room. He hung up his jacket and hovered near her shoulder while she laid out the place mats and tableware.

"So," he asked, leaning forward for her answer, smiling his crooked smile, "how was it? I already know you were the prettiest girl in the class. Were you the smartest too? Are you going to be teacher's pet?"

She felt a stab of anger at the mention of the teacher, but she managed a smile while he waited for a reply. "I'm not the smartest girl in the class, but it was fine. It'll take me a while to get back into the rhythm of class work and studying."

"What classes are you taking?" he asked while removing his tie and unbuttoning the top button of his shirt. "Did you decide to pick up chemistry again? As I recall, Emma says you were Sam's best student." He winked lasciviously. "In more ways than one."

She ignored his joke. "Just one. World Literature. Perhaps I'll take something in the sciences next semester."

"I thought you were going to start with your required courses."

"I was, but Biochemistry two-oh-one was filled," she replied, still uneasy. "I'll take it next semester. Or maybe next fall."

Wesley hooted out loud. "Biochemistry two-oh-one? Just wait. You'll get old Professor Sloan. He's been there forever, and he'll bore you to death. He thinks everyone loves chemistry the way he does." He laughed again. "It'll be a long semester."

"Oh, I'm sure it'll be just fine. Right now I'm looking forward to the World Lit with Professor Corrigan. I'll let you know how it goes."

Wanting this line of conversation to end, she turned her attention to Emma in the kitchen. "Where's my dinner? I've had a hard day of school, and I'm starved."

CHAPTER FOUR

World Literature proved to be a complete pleasure. Paula mentally thanked her advisor for suggesting it. Professor Corrigan, an ageless dynamo who lived and breathed the subject, brought fire and drama to the text. Literature of any kind had always been one of her favorites. Energized by the topic, she always left class in high spirits. Outside reading was heavy but thoroughly enjoyable. As her confidence grew, she began to participate in class discussions, sometimes even offering her opinion.

To her surprise, she was accepted by the younger students as if she were one of them, and she was happy to note the presence of other mature students, some almost as mature as she. She wasn't such an anomaly at all. She made a mental note to tell Emma. At the end of the second week, she felt comfortable and looked forward to the rest of the semester.

At the end of class on the second Friday, she stopped by the Chemistry Department office on her way home. It was late in the day, and she was sure everyone would have left except for Lottie Brannigan, the department secretary. Outside of Ed King and his wife, Lottie was the only member of the department Paula had ever gotten to know, and she valued the pleasurable hours they had spent over a cup of tea. Lottie was the closest thing to a friend that Paula had known since she and Sam had been married.

Lottie would know the next semester's teacher assignments, therefore how long Paula would have to wait to take 201 without Boyd Mackenzie standing at the head of the class. She would be able to plan the next couple of terms around that information.

"Well, if it isn't my favorite faculty wife," Lottie welcomed warmly when Paula stuck her head in the door. "Come on in and have a cup of tea. I was about to put the kettle on."

She raised her portly body from her desk and opened her arms, a broad smile on her round face. Paula dropped her books on the desk and embraced Lottie. "A cup of Earl Gray would save my life right now. I'm wasted."

She followed Lottie into the faculty lounge at the back of the office where soft leather sofas and well-used armchairs invited her to sit and put up her feet. The kettle whistled almost immediately, and Lottie dropped teabags into an ancient brown betty. While the tea steeped, a homemade coffee cake appeared from the depths of the pantry, along with thick clotted cream from the tiny refrigerator. Lottie, always the miracle worker, for which Paula was grateful.

Calm environment, treasured company, and strong tea restored her equilibrium. She slipped off her shoes and curled up on the sofa as Lottie poured the hot, fragrant liquid into mismatched china cups worn thin over the years by the many hands that had handled them. Lottie put all the telephones on voice mail, settled herself into a luxurious armchair, and placed a large piece of coffee cake on her saucer. She pushed a lock of steel-gray hair behind her ear and leaned forward to focus on Paula.

"Tell me, love, how are your classes going? It must be exciting to go back to school after being a housewife for so long. I envy you, I do."

Paula sighed. "Oh yes, it's exciting, and my World Lit class is very interesting."

"Professor Corrigan?"

Paula nodded, her mouth full of cake.

Lottie sipped her tea thoughtfully. "Ah, yes, he's in love with his subject, they say. So you're becoming a student again."

"Actually, it's more than that. It feels like I've become a real person. It's been so long since someone called me Paula instead of Mrs. Wincott, I'd forgotten what it was like."

"I hope you noticed that you're not the only grown-up student in your class. Professor Corrigan is a big draw for mature students as well as the youngsters."

"I thought I'd be the only doddering ancient in class, but there are a few of us." She took a long sip of tea and laid her head back against the chair while the stresses of the day slipped away.

"How about the chemistry course?" Lottie prodded. "I found your name on Professor Mackenzie's class roll. Isn't he a dream? My knees go weak every time he comes into the office. He's been in the department ten years, and I still can't get used to how handsome he is."

Although Paula's body stiffened, she replied coolly, "Oh, I really didn't notice his looks." Ignoring Lottie's oblique look, she continued, "And I don't know that he's such a good teacher either. As a matter of fact, I dropped his class."

"Oh?"

For some reason, Lottie's tone put her on the defensive. "The class time didn't fit my schedule, and he didn't seem quite right for lower level courses."

"That's too bad," Lottie observed, tilting her head to one side. "His reputation as a teacher is equal to his reputation as a researcher. He's known for his patience and care for his students." She popped a piece of cake into her mouth and washed it down with tea before asking, "Couldn't you rearrange your schedule? You'd benefit from taking a class with him."

"No," Paula replied, unease growing. She didn't like the direction the conversation was taking.

Seemingly unaware of Paula's discomfort, Lottie continued, "Maybe another time. I really think you should consider his class."

Paula was about to snap a sharp reply when she heard footsteps in the outer office followed by, "Lottie, my fine beauty, I've come to abduct you and carry you off on my camel."

Lottie's face took on a girlish glow. "Well, speak of the devil." She raised her head and called out, "Back here, Dr. Mackenzie. We're taking a tea break. Come and have a sit down with us."

Paula hadn't anticipated running into a faculty member at this time of day. And this particular one was most certainly not welcome. But Lottie turned to Paula with a smile as she reached for another cup and saucer.

Paula's heart fell as he stepped through the doorway, looming tall and handsome. He seemed to pause for a beat, and, she noted with satisfaction, appeared surprised to see her with Lottie.

Then, he obviously regained his composure and grinned. "Lottie, my love, how are you this beautiful day? You look wonderful, as usual. When are you going to let me take you away from all this?" He winked broadly and waggled his eyebrows.

"Oh, you silver-tongued charmer, you're too beguiling by half, don't you know! You'd best be careful; someday I just might take you up on your offer. And then where would you be?"

Lottie put down her cup and reached for the teapot. "But in the meantime, won't you join us in a cup of tea? Have you met Paula Wincott? I think she signed up for your two-oh-one section but had scheduling conflicts."

Boyd cast a fleeting look at Paula. "Mrs. Wincott. Good afternoon," he greeted her formally, then spoke to Lottie, a warmth in his tone, "Thanks, but I'm in a rush today. I came in to see if my exam papers are ready."

"Yes, indeed. They're done and waiting for you. I locked them away in my desk. Have a cup of tea, while I get them for you." She stood and gestured to an empty chair. "Here, take a seat and chat with Paula."

Paula shot him a warning glance as he backed out of the room. "Another time, if you please. I'll just pick up my exams and be on my way."

"You must at least take a piece of my special coffee cake," Lottie urged, quickly cutting a large slice and wrapping it in a paper napkin. "You're always in such a rush, and you don't eat nearly enough."

He accepted the cake with a slight bow. "You're the best, Lottie. Thanks very much." Without a word to Paula, he moved to the outer office to pick up his papers.

Lottie followed to unlock the desk for him, then returned to the lounge while he gathered his papers. She looked askance at Paula. "He called you Mrs. Wincott?"

Paula shrugged. "Yes."

"Nobody calls anyone by their surname around here. Why so formal?"

Squirming in her seat, Paula thought fast. "We've never met before. And I'm sure he regards me purely as Sam's wife."

"You know, that's right," Lottie replied, a slight furrow in her brow. "You never came around much, and you never attended any of department functions. I guess there are a lot of faculty members you don't know."

"Sam always said he preferred to go alone—or

not at all—so he could leave when he got bored," Paula explained. "He was dedicated to his work, and he thought faculty gatherings were frivolous."

"I guess I never thought about it, but the tea times we've had over the years have always been late in the afternoon when you'd been shopping or on your way home. Always in a hurry. Why was that?"

"Oh, I don't know, just busy with home and family, I guess," Paula hedged, holding up her saucer. "Could I have another tiny piece of cake?"

As Boyd left, he called out, "Lottie, I promise I'll eat quite enough at the faculty dinner on Saturday, and, oh, Mrs. Wincott, I'm looking forward to seeing you there."

Beneath a cold shower of dread, Paula recalled the upcoming dinner. As a faculty wife, she had always been invited to the dinners, but had never attended. Now that Sam was gone, Dr. King insisted she attend as a tribute to Sam. Since all the faculty was invited, and she would certainly run into Boyd Mackenzie.

"Why, what's wrong, dear?" Lottie patted her hand. "You look ill. Don't you like my coffee cake?"

"You know I adore your coffee cake, but I just remembered I have a few important errands to run, and it's getting late."

"Just like I said," Lottie sighed. "Always in a hurry."

Paula reached for her shoes and handbag. "I promise I'll stop in again very soon." She gathered her books from the desk in the front office. "Thanks for the tea and chat."

Lottie called a cheery good-bye, "Don't be a stranger," and poured herself another cup of tea.

****

Paula considered a dozen reasons not to attend the faculty dinner, but by the time Saturday arrived, none was good enough. So, she decided to put on her war paint and beard the lion in his den.

She shopped for hours until she found just the right dress, a dark green jersey with long sleeves and a square neckline. The skirt, cut on the bias, draped diagonally across her hips and floated to the floor. It suited her hourglass figure perfectly, and the look gave her much-needed confidence. Although she was sure Emma would not approve, she brushed a bit of green shadow over her lids, daubed an earth-tone lipstick on her still-full lips, and flicked dark brown mascara on her lashes. Sam's last gift to her, pearls clustered on golden chains, hung from her ears. She felt a tiny stab of pain that he was gone from her forever. But she was Mrs. Sam Wincott, and she would do him proud.

When she reached the dining hall of the faculty club, she was relieved to find Ed King approaching, arms outstretched. "Paula, I was beginning to think we would never see you at one of these dinners." He took her wrap, then grasped her hands. "Thank you for being here. I'm sure Sam would be so happy."

She relaxed a little and determined to enjoy the evening.

"Thank you for considering me a faculty wife though, strictly speaking, I'm not truly a wife anymore. I know Sam would appreciate your kindness."

"No kindness at all. You'll always be one of us."

He took her arm and steered her from group to group, introducing her as Sam's wife. She had never met most of the other faculty members, and she found them warm and welcoming, not at all the tedious lot that Sam had so often described.

When dinner was announced, Ed appeared at her elbow. "I've had you seated next to me. I've been wanting to talk to you about something important, and this seemed like the perfect opportunity. Helen's spending the weekend with the kids, so you and I can have a serious discussion. After dinner, of course."

"You sound positively cryptic. Are you sending me on a spying mission?"

He tapped his forefinger against his nose and nodded. "Something even better."

He led her to a long table that seated about twenty people, faculty members and spouses she had never met. But all of them seemed genuinely interested in her, and conversation flowed easily.

Dinner was a delicious mix of seafood and Mediterranean dishes, and, although she normally didn't drink wine, she allowed herself to be coaxed into a glass of excellent dry white. With the delightful wine came a measure of calm that allowed her to remain cool when she spied Boyd at the far end of the table, engaged in earnest conversation with Dr. Marvin Shilcroft, Professor Emeritus and close friend of Sam's. Boyd seemed not to have noticed her presence, and she relaxed.

Ed waited until dessert and coffee arrived before broaching the topic he had promised. As the waiter poured coffee, he turned to her. "So, you're back in school."

"Hardly back in school. I'm taking one course, just to test the waters."

"Lottie tells me you registered for Biochemistry."

She didn't want to open this line of conversation. "I did, but it conflicted with the English courses I was interested in, so I decided to wait until the spring semester."

"But you always had a special affinity for chemistry."

She gave him a merry look. "What I had was a *special affinity* for the chemistry professor those many years ago."

"Speaking of that professor, how much do you know about the project Sam was working on just before he passed away?"

"You mean his research? I didn't know about it first hand, but he talked a lot about it at home," she replied, pouring cream into her coffee. "He was working extra hard and putting in a lot of hours, even at night, but he believed it was very important. He said it was going to be bigger than Teflon."

Ed nodded and passed the sugar bowl. "Yes, he felt DuPont had been unfair in not giving Dr. Park, the Teflon developer, financial credit for such a significant achievement. Joe Park worked here for many years, you know. He and Sam had long conversations about it."

He looked directly at her. "Did you understand the chemical processes Sam studied, the experiments he ran?"

She took a sip of coffee before answering. "I can't say I understood all of it. I didn't study upper level chemistry, but inorganic was always my strong suit."

"So I've been told," he agreed. "You might have made a fine lab partner if you had continued your studies."

She let his remark sink in for a moment. "I know he was working on the technology of high polymers—more importantly, conductive polymers, but I don't know any of the details. I assumed it had something to do with communications technology, but I left all of that to Sam."

"That's right," Ed said, as if he'd had a sudden flash of recall. "He was working on new applications of resin polymers in conductivity and fire retardants."

"He said he was breaking new ground."

"Well, he was naturally disappointed that Alan Heeger's inorganic group beat him to the Nobel Prize, but that didn't stop him from continuing his work. He was working diligently, and the few times I talked with him, he seemed excited about recent successes in the lab."

"Did he tell you much about it?"

Ed smiled. "No, he didn't leak much information, and I couldn't wheedle it from him."

"That was my Sam," she chuckled. "He always played it close to the vest."

He turned his chair to face her. "Sam's goal, of course, was not only development but also publication, and I really want his work to continue."

"Of course. We all do."

"We've recruited a savvy young fellow from the University of Wisconsin to take over the lab next fall. He's everything we've been looking for since Sam passed, but next fall is a long time away."

She nodded in agreement. "It is indeed, but the work won't be delayed, will it?"

"Not the work itself," he reassured her. "In the interim, we need someone to coordinate daily administration of Sam's lab. It doesn't require a great deal of expertise in inorganic chemistry." He took a deep breath. "Would you be willing to help us out? It would really mean helping Sam."

She almost choked on the bite of crème bruleé she had just put in her mouth. "Me?" She hastily swallowed. "Ed, surely you're joking. I'm just a wife, not a chemist."

"Who better to be the standard bearer for his work than his lifetime partner, the woman he loved? And you don't have to carry out the experiments. We already have his grad students in place, and they're happy to continue his work with Barry Connors supervising. All we need is someone to monitor their hours for the payroll, keep track of expenditures, someone who knew Sam well enough to know exactly how he would want his lab to be run."

Looking like a man who had just accomplished the coup of the century, he sat back. "That's you."

"But, Ed, I've been a wife and mother all these

years. How could the students respect me as a colleague? They know more than I do." She gave him a wry grin. "Virtually anyone knows more than I do."

"Sure, they know more about chemistry than you," he agreed. "They know enough to do the work, but you know more about Sam and his goals than anyone."

Ed could be very convincing when he applied himself, and Paula found him troweling on the charm. "I'm asking you as a personal favor. Please help our department support Sam's plans. Lottie could set you up on the office payroll, and you could make your own hours."

Ed had placed her squarely on the horns of a dilemma. She felt inadequate to the task, yet maybe, just maybe she could accomplish it—with the right kind of assistance. And wouldn't it be a thrill to actually help bring Sam's vision to light? She toyed with her spoon while she considered Ed's plea. Could she possibly serve the project adequately? He seemed to think so, but she was unsure. She had never even been in Sam's lab.

Ed threw the clincher. "I'd hate to close down the lab just when the research efforts are about to pay off."

"No, you can't close down his work! Sam always said they were creating major inroads in telecommunications."

He eyed her keenly. "All right, help me to help Sam."

"How?"

"What do you know about how his lab functioned? I've talked to the students, but they know only the individual experiments they've been running."

She paused to think for a second. "Sam always spoke about needing more help, a few more grad students to stagger hours and keep the work moving steadily. Could we do that? He was so frustrated because there was never enough money."

"My dear, money will not be a problem. I know just the person to get us all the government grants we'll ever need."

He made a signaling motion with one hand. "Let me introduce you to the golden boy of grant writing. He practically mints money."

****

Boyd puzzled over Dr. King's hand gesture. He had hoped for the opportunity to confront Paula again, but this didn't seem like the time. Perhaps he could chance it. Surely she wouldn't snap at him in front of the chairman of the department.

Unsure of the reason behind the summons, he excused himself to Professor Shilcroft then made his way to where Dr. King and Paula waited.

He stood at the edge of the table. "Good evening, Ed. You wanted to see me?"

"Ah, yes, I'd like to introduce you to Paula, Sam Wincott's wife," Ed opened. "We've just been having a fascinating conversation, and we need your input, if you don't mind."

Paula did not raise her eyes as the introduction was made, but Boyd countered quickly, "Mrs. Wincott and I have met." He looked directly at her. "How nice to see you again."

His smile was guarded as he waited, forcing her hand. Good manners prevailed; at last, she looked up to acknowledge him. "Professor Mackenzie," was all she said, but Boyd caught the quick rise and fall of her bosom above the square cut of her neckline and an angry flush on her cheek.

Ed reached behind him to snag another chair, pulled it close, then gestured for Boyd to sit. "My boy, Paula and I need your help." He then outlined the plan for continuing Sam's pet project and the need for financial aid to support the research and the student technicians.

Boyd listened attentively, occasionally nodding, asked a few pertinent questions and was satisfied with Ed's answers.

"With your government connections and your excellent relations with the funding organizations," Ed concluded, "with your skills at grant writing, you're just the one to come on board."

Boyd couldn't have been more surprised. Or intrigued.

He stole a glance at Paula, then cleared his throat. "Ed, I have only rudimentary knowledge of inorganic chemistry. I wouldn't even know what to put in the grant proposal. I don't believe I'd be very effective."

"Oh, don't worry about that part," Ed scoffed. "The lab students can give you all the pertinents, and Paula can give you the overall picture. Sam shared his goals with her, if not the details of his work, so she's in the loop."

Boyd was not convinced. "I don't think I'm the right person to do this. I think you should get a professional grant writer who knows more about Sam's work, someone who's up on the technology."

He didn't want to work with Paula in such a potentially volatile environment. Better shut down this line of conversation cleanly. "I know a couple of top notch guys I could refer you to. Let me get you a contact number. I'll even give them a call for you."

Ed slapped him on the shoulder. "I think you're the top notch guy."

"I'm flattered, but I don't see how I could do the project justice."

"Why don't you two get together and sort it all out," Ed suggested, "then have a talk with Sam's current project leader, Barry Connors. I'm sure he can bring you up to speed. This would mean so much to the department and, of course, to Paula."

33

Boyd caught her eye, hoping she would refuse the offer so he would be off the hook. He was happy to write the proposal for Sam, but putting his widow into the mix could prove devastating. He didn't want to be party to another blow-up.

"What can I say?" he vamped, waiting for her to refuse outright.

She came to his aid. "I'm sure Professor Mackenzie has more than enough on his plate without having to take on such a large responsibility, especially in an area where he has no expertise."

"He's the best in the business," Ed assured her. "He can do this in his sleep, can't you, Boyd?"

Boyd saw that she had no intention of working with him, nor did he want to continue with this line of conversation. He was thrown when she suddenly acquiesced.

"All right, Ed," she said. "I don't believe it'll work, but we'll talk about it. You understand I won't make any guarantees."

Ed laughed off her reservations. "Of course. But I have no doubt that you two can make it work."

Without looking at him and with ice in her tone, she spoke perfunctorily to Boyd, "Why don't you call me, and we'll discuss the idea." She signaled the waiter for more coffee.

Boyd had been dismissed.

Relieved but irritated at her curtness, he stood to take his leave, only to be tapped on the shoulder by a curvaceous young brunette. "Come and dance with me," she cajoled, tossing wild curls over her shoulder. "My husband can't rumba. Actually he hates dancing."

Boyd turned to Sam and Paula. "If you will excuse me?"

Without waiting for acknowledgement, he swept the young woman into a close embrace and moved smoothly onto the dance floor.

Ed turned to Paula with a smile as he poured more wine into her glass. "I think that went rather well, don't you?"

CHAPTER FIVE

The next morning found Paula in her robe and slippers and making coffee when the doorbell rang. She peeked out the kitchen window but saw no one at the door. She padded to the front door to look through the peephole. Boyd Mackenzie loomed large in the tiny fisheye glass. How dare he show up at her house!

He rang the bell again. She still didn't answer. Instead, she returned to the kitchen and finished filling the coffeepot. He could ring the bell forever. She would ignore him for longer. The dark-brewed coffee was filling the carafe when tapping sounded at the kitchen door. She looked up to see him grinning at her through the glass panes of the French door. "Good morning. I guess you didn't hear me at the front door."

Without moving, she shouted back, "What are you doing here?"

"You forgot to give me your telephone number," he continued, still at full volume, "so I came in person. May I come in?"

"No, you may not. Go away!"

"Not until we talk, so you might as well open the door. Or should we share our conversation with the neighbors? I can stand out here and talk. Loudly, if you want." The man was nothing if not relentless.

She didn't know which prospect was worse: having the neighbors hear them quarreling or opening the door and allowing Sam's arch enemy inside her home. In the end, she took the line of least resistance. She tied her robe tightly around her waist, jerked the door open, and glared at him.

His eyes twinkled at this small capitulation, but he kept a straight face. "Thank you, Mrs. Wincott, and fine good morning to you, too."

The impertinent way he had of emphasizing *Mrs. Wincott* brought a sharp reaction from her. Sensing he was baiting her, she ignored him.

She moved aside to allow him entry; he took a seat at the end of the kitchen table. She had no choice but to look at him, and what she saw annoyed her. He looked relaxed and casual in snug jeans and a blue pullover sweater the exact color of his eyes. His smile was compelling. He could sell toothpaste with that full mouth and those straight white teeth.

"Is that coffee I smell?" He turned a bland face to her. "If you don't mind, maybe I could have a cup while we talk?"

She crossed her arms and refused to move. "There's nothing to talk about. We are not going to work together. I'm not even sure I can help with Sam's project. You've wasted your time showing up here."

"You agreed last night that we would talk, and Ed is expecting us to come to an understanding about how to move forward with grants for the lab to remain in operation until the new guy comes on board. I tried to get out of this, but you agreed."

"I thought it was obvious my agreement to talk was only to shut Ed down. It appears we are talking right now, but you must know any collaboration between us is impossible. We are *not* going to work together. Forget the coffee and take yourself out of here."

He leaned his elbows on the table, then narrowed his gaze. "We could have coffee while you tell me how we're not going to work together and why you don't want to publish Sam's work."

His dart found its mark. After a momentary

standoff, she snorted loudly and pulled two mugs from the cupboard. She placed one smartly in front of him and poured the fresh-brewed coffee. She took her cup and sat at the other end of the table, mind racing. Of course she wanted to publish Sam's work. What kind of a wife did he think she was? But the last person she wanted to collaborate with was sitting across the table from her.

She waited in stubborn silence for him to take a long pull of coffee. Then, jaw firmly set, he sat forward to face her. "Let's begin again, shall we? And talk as two people with a common goal. Sam was a fine man, a brilliant scholar. I admired him, and am happy to do what I can with my limited talents. But I'm not here to fight, and will not allow you to insult me any further. Now, do you want my help or not?"

She held her cup tightly, trying to sort out conflicting emotions. Yes, she wanted his help, but didn't like the ground rules that required her to see and speak to him. There had to be a way out of the trap.

He took another sip of coffee and sat back in his chair, watching and waiting. Long moments passed while Paula considered the options. After a painful exploration of possibilities, she realized she had none. Reluctantly, and certainly without grace, she accepted the inevitable. She could accept Boyd's help with financing or forget about Sam's project.

"If you put it that way, I guess I don't have any choice. But understand this: I'm doing this for my husband, and it's a temporary truce only." She pushed off a curl of hair from her forehead, eyed him carefully. "Where do we go from here?"

Clearly he was ready. "First, I want a list of the students already working in the lab. I'll need to know how many more students would provide the full head count. Barry can sit down with me and describe in detail just what they're doing. I can write the rest. Do you know how much money the lab needs? And what kind of equipment?"

"No," she admitted. "I really don't know much of anything about that yet, but I can find out. Lottie will have a list of the students already working on the project, and I'll talk to Barry Connors about how many more students we'll need. You can talk to him about the details of the work. He'll also know the approximate financial shortfall. Sam was always in need of more funding. He complained about that all the time."

Yes, he had complained more than once that his lab was chronically under funded while Boyd Mackenzie's coffers were always filled with gold. He seemed to take it personally, as if there were some sort of conspiracy to deny him his due. She felt a familiar stab of sympathy for the injustice of the situation. Now at last, the playing field would be level. The same man who had cheated Sam of his standing at the university would be responsible for restoring it to him. She wished he could be here to enjoy the irony.

"Okay." Boyd drained his cup and rose from the table. "We'll get started tomorrow. What time can you be available to meet?"

Irritated at his presumption, she dug in her heels. "Not tomorrow."

"Then, when?"

"Didn't we just meet?" she snapped. "What more do you want from me?"

"You and I will have to get together with Connors and go through the specifics of the research so I can be pro-active in preparing the grant proposals. Then, you will have to fill me in on Sam's personal thoughts. There might be some hook I can use, something he mentioned to you but not to his students, to push the proposals to the head of the line, something that makes them stand out as special."

"Special? In what way?"

"I'd like to tell them something of the man himself."

He opened the French door and stood on the threshold. "We'll be seeing a lot of each other."

He turned back to her with a genuine smile. "Get used to it."

CHAPTER SIX

Paula shared the news with Emma on the telephone that afternoon. "Oh, Mom, that's wonderful. You must be so excited," she responded cheerfully. "But why would Dr. King ask you to work on Dad's project? You don't know anything about his work." As an afterthought, she said, "I mean, you didn't even finish college."

The edge in Emma's voice, a tone that had become more common in the past year, made Paula want to defend herself. "I wouldn't say I don't know anything about his work. I was an A student in chemistry years ago, and your father talked about his work with me all the time. You might say I was his confidante."

"Yes, but—"

Wanting to end the conversation on a happy note, Paula said, "Barry Connors will be heading up the research lab. I'll monitor hours, hire additional staff, and keep everyone and everything moving. Dr. King thought it would be a tribute to your father that I, as Sam's wife, assisted in the publication of his research."

"Oh, I definitely agree," Emma conceded. "Dad's work should be published. And I think it would be a great way for you to occupy your time. You said you felt at loose ends; this is such a worthwhile undertaking." Her voice took on a conciliatory tone. "Now you don't have to take all those courses and worry about getting a silly old degree. This is much more important. I know Dad would agree."

Emma had a way of bringing every conversation

into line with her own way of thinking, but Paula wasn't ready to cave in just yet. "Oh, I don't believe it'll be necessary for me to give up my coursework, especially since I'm enjoying my World Lit so much. I have lots of time, and don't forget, the grad students will actually be doing the work. I'm sure I can manage things just fine."

"But Mom—"

"Don't worry about me. Give the kids a kiss from their Nana, and I'll talk to you later in the week." She hung up before Emma could get in another word.

****

After turning in her first paper in her literature class on Monday morning, Paula headed out the side door, across the lawn, past the fountain, and made her way to the Chemistry Building. Inside, the beehive of activity exhilarated her. She stopped the first student she saw and asked where Dr. Wincott's lab was located. When she stuck her head inside the door, she was greeted by a tall blond student in a white lab coat.

"May I help you?"

He was a fresh-faced lad of indeterminate age. To Paula they all looked to be no more than sixteen. She suddenly felt very old and out of place, but she pressed forward, hoping he wouldn't notice her discomfort.

"Good morning; I'm Paula Wincott. Aren't you Barry Connors?" she ventured cautiously. "You're one of my husband's research assistants, I think. He's mentioned you many times."

His face broke into a cheery grin, and he offered his hand. "Oh, Mrs. Wincott, how do you do. I'm happy to meet you. Professor Mackenzie was just here and explained that we'll all be working together for the next few months. We're all revved."

So Boyd had been here ahead of her. He

certainly didn't waste any time. "Yes, I'm sure," she responded dryly.

"We're really lucky to have Professor Mackenzie on the team. We've just about run out of everything, and we really need new equipment. We've been flying on a wing and a prayer, as my granddad used to say."

She shook his hand while he chatted on. "I think this is just the shot in the arm we've needed for a long time."

"Really? I didn't know you needed money that urgently."

"Frankly, I was afraid we'd have to shut down our operation completely, but now with Professor Mackenzie on the team I'm optimistic that we'll have enough money to buy everything we need. We might even be able to pay the assistants' back salaries. What a surprise that would be."

His good humor reminded her of Wesley, and she liked him immediately. At the same time she was dismayed to hear how near they were to curtailing their work. Maybe they really did need someone like Boyd Mackenzie. Someone like him— anyone like him—just not Boyd Mackenzie himself.

Barry offered to show her around the lab, pointing out work in progress, other work on hold until more money could be found, and finally showed her to a cubicle holding veritable mountains of paperwork scattered here and there, some in clumps, others spread in single sheets, but altogether a mess of disjointed notes.

"Here's where you can really help," he pointed out in earnest. "We just don't have the time or manpower to sort this all out and put it in order, and we really need to refer to our notes on at least a weekly basis, preferably daily."

"I'm sure." She couldn't believe Sam's lab could be in such disarray. It wasn't like him.

"It's not a pretty job, and I hate to ask, but how would you feel about taking a look at it? You don't have to answer right away."

Her heart sank as she took in the rat's nest of papers. She knew Sam loved the work but not the paperwork. He always relied on clerical staff to keep that part of the lab in order. He had always given high points to neatness, and she was surprised to see the gross clutter throughout the cubicle. Clearly, the lab was in need of help, hers as well as Boyd's. She felt a sense of purpose, certainly equal to that of Boyd Mackenzie.

"Sure, I'd be happy to help," she offered. "I'll set up a schedule so that I'm not in your way, and see what I can do to put this in some kind of order. I can't guarantee I'll understand it, but I can at least put it in chronological order and make a few binders, then we'll decide where to put it so anyone who needs to reference it will find it. We'll encourage everyone to add their notes to the appropriate binders at the end of each lab session. How would that be?"

Barry looked overwhelmed. "Wow, that would be just great, Mrs. Wincott. I can't believe our good luck. You're just what the doctor ordered."

"Dr. King, to be exact," she quipped. "And please call me Paula. We're going to be seeing a lot of each other, and there's no sense standing on formality. Now, if you'll leave me to my own devices, I'll roll up my sleeves and get started right now."

"Sure thing."

He pointed behind her. "The coffee pot is over there, the water fountain is just outside the door, and the ladies' room is down the hall. I'll introduce you to Amy Billings when she comes in. She worked very closely with Professor Wincott, and I'm sure she'll welcome you to the team. Oh, and we usually order pizza around seven o'clock—if you happen to be working that late."

"Oh, I think I can guarantee that," she assured him.

He flashed a grin and retired to his work table, relief evident in his face.

After several hours, she realized she had a prodigious amount of work ahead of her. Since the only way to eat an elephant was one bite at a time, she packed up as many papers as fit in her briefcase and gathered her books. She waved to the dark-haired, pony-tailed girl, Amy, who after being introduced, dug into her own work and seldom looked up after that.

"I'll be in again tomorrow."

Amy nodded, and continued her calculations.

That night Paula spent hours sorting papers—on the floor, dining room table, buffet, anywhere she found a flat surface. She made no attempt to determine the content of the work. At this point, putting the dates in order was enough. When her vision blurred and her head began to ache, she gave herself permission to relax in a hot tub then tumbled into a soft bed. She felt exhausted but wonderful. She was needed. Her work had value. And Emma would approve. For the first time in a year, she slept peacefully and soundly.

****

The next couple of weeks flew by. She stopped at Sam's lab each day to pick up another satchel of papers. Every night she sat up late sorting and arranging them in chronological order. In a way, the activity kept her in touch with Sam, something she had been sorely missing. Her contribution was important to the project and she saw the results of improved organization start to show. A couple of times she passed Boyd either going or coming, knowing he was meeting with Barry Connors about the details of the grant proposal. He remained unfailingly courteous; she was barely civil.

One morning, she literally bumped into him on her way out of the lab. His face lit up when he saw her. "Paula," he began. "Mrs. Wincott," he amended amiably. "Exactly the person I need to see. I've been talking to Barry, and I pretty much have the scientific details in order. Now I just need to sit down with you and get some idea of what Sam was about. I need to put a face on this proposal."

His face was sober, but his eyes still smiled. "Why don't I take you for that belated cup of coffee? We can run over to the cafeteria. It won't take long." His eyes almost dared her to decline.

She had dreaded this moment, but was ready. Without missing a beat, she accepted the dare. "I think that's an excellent idea. Now is as good a time as any."

Without waiting for him to lead the way, she turned quickly to the back door of the Chemistry Building which led outside into the fountain area. She shielded her eyes against the bright Colorado sun, allowing it to warm her spirits. Boyd caught up beside her but offered no conversation.

Once inside the cafeteria, he angled his head in the direction of a nearby table. "Why don't you take my briefcase and grab that table while I get the coffee? I'll be just be a minute." Without waiting for a response, he handed her the briefcase, then turned to the coffee urn.

As she set both briefcases on a nearby table, female voices trilled from across the room, "Oh, Professor Mackenzie, over here."

She recognized two young students from the Biochemistry 201 class. They waved their arms, attempting to attract his attention. She studied them for a moment. Over-processed hair, far too much make-up, and clothing that left nothing to the imagination. And, the most damning aspect, one of them bore a suggestive tattoo on one bare shoulder. Paula couldn't tell from a distance, but she wondered if the other girl had a tattoo as well, possibly in a less noticeable area of the body.

"Professor Mackenzie, here. Come and sit with us," begged the plump blonde. "We have some...uhm...chemistry-related questions." She broke into giggles while her brunette friend slapped her arm to shush her.

Boyd heard them just as he picked up the tray laden with coffee and Danish pastry, shook his head, and pointed to Paula. The two girls followed his hand signal and gave her puzzled looks, then shrugged. Paula pretended not to notice, but another burst of titters put her teeth on edge.

"Here we are."

He set coffee and pastry in front of her, but instead of seating himself across the table from her, pulled up a chair next to her. He smelled the scent of her shampoo, clean and fresh, not heavy with exotic scent like other women he had known. Her green eyes crinkled at the corners, and he considered that she might have a pleasing smile. Not that he had ever seen her smile.

He took a quick swallow of black coffee, then pulled out his legal pad and a pen and gave her an open look betraying nothing, pen posed over the paper. "Why don't I ask some questions; you can fill me in on any details you think might be important. As I said, Barry and the other students have been very helpful, and, if you can give me a couple of hours, I think I can get all the information I need to put this to bed."

"I understand," she replied, stirring sugar into her coffee. "I don't have a couple hours, so let's get on with it."

She took a bite of the pastry, and a bit of red jelly found its way to her upper lip. It struck Boyd as pleasantly incongruous in a woman so full of bitterness. "What do you need to know exactly?"

She looked up, and this time there was no overt animosity in her shuttered gaze. She was just a woman with jelly on her mouth, and he found her disarming.

"Let's begin with Sam. What kind of man was he? Outside the lab, I mean. What was important to him? I'm trying to get a picture of the man himself. So I can present him in the best light, you understand."

"Do you mean his personal life?"

"Whatever you think would be pertinent,"

After a long moment, she said, "My husband was a very complex man, really. He was a brilliant scientist, but you already know that. He was dedicated to his work, highly respected, certainly a workaholic. I guess you know that, too. There were many nights the children and I ate dinner without him, and we often went to bed before he got home."

Her tongue slipped out and caught the jelly on the tip, rolled over her top lip, and slid back into her mouth. "But," she continued, "He was also a wonderful husband and father. He adored his family and always knew exactly what was best for us, even if we didn't. Is that what you mean?"

Green eyes met blue in a questioning look that held for a long moment.

Shifting uncomfortably, Boyd gripped his coffee mug. "Yes, of course that... and what benefit he thought his work would bring to society at large. Did he talk about how he felt about his work in the larger context of making a positive contribution to the world? That's what's going to look good in the grant proposal. I want to paint a picture of a selfless, philanthropic scientist, someone with a human side. His work speaks for itself, but I didn't know him outside of the department. That's why I have to rely on you."

He realized he was rattling, but wanted to keep her talking, if only to hear the soft cadence of her voice. Had they met under alternative circumstances, he might have found her charming.

"I don't know what else I can tell you. He had so many wonderful attributes."

"Okay, let's see. How about his home life? For example, how did you meet?"

"I was his student. We fell in love almost at first sight. He was already famous, and I felt so special when he chose me. It was like a fairy tale, you know; Prince Charming picked Cinderella, sort of."

For a moment, her face took on a far away look. "It feels like such a short time ago, not thirty-two years." She came back to the present with a start. "You won't put that in the prospectus, are you?"

"No, no, of course not. I was just trying to get an idea of the personal side of the man. As I said, I knew him only as a professional colleague, and he was very reserved, like many researchers."

He scribbled something on the notepad, then asked without looking up, "And you have children I believe? Any other scientists in the family?"

"We have a son and a daughter, but neither was interested in chemistry, or in any of the sciences for that matter. Sam had always hoped our son would follow in his footsteps, but Morgan is a free spirit. He lives in Switzerland and flies all over the world for his import/export business."

"I can see you're very proud of your son."

"Our daughter Emma lives here in Boulder with her husband. They've given me two beautiful grandchildren who are the lights of my life."

Her voice took on a bitter tone. "They never got to spend much time with Sam; he was always so busy. He would have gotten to know them better if he had lived, but he was taken away so

49

unexpectedly. It wasn't fair to him or his family."

"I'm very sorry." He wanted to say more, offer condolences, but he couldn't find the words.

Her cell phone rang. She looked at the caller ID and gave Boyd a wry look. "That's my grandchildren now," she said curtly. "I promised I'd take them on a picnic to Bluebell Canyon on Saturday, so we have to make plans. Are we finished here?"

He gathered up his pad and paper. "For now. I'll call you if I need anything else. Thank you for your time."

He zipped up his satchel and left her sitting at the table, by now totally immersed in her telephone conversation. She hadn't been warm and agreeable, but at least she wasn't yelling at him.

CHAPTER SEVEN

After picking up her first English paper on Friday, Paula stopped by Sam's lab to deliver the most recent stack of work and pick up another batch of notes and charts from the overcrowded cubicle. She decided it would be a good time to check the hours the students had racked up and put them in order pending the outcome of the grant applications.

As she crossed the threshold, Barry met her with a grin that stretched almost all the way around his head. "Paula, come in. You'll never guess what!"

"I'll bite. What?"

He took the briefcase from her and grasped both her hands in his. "We got some money! Isn't that great? Look at all this cool stuff."

"What do you mean you got some money? What money?" she asked. "Where did it come from? As far as I know, the grant applications haven't even been written yet. In fact, we're still putting together information."

"Come on, let me show you." He took her arm and walked her around the lab, pointing out several cheerful grad students working with obviously new, upgraded equipment. "We got a little bridge financing to tide us over until the big money comes in," he continued. "We even got some of our back pay. Whew, what a relief."

"You did?"

"Now we can continue the work without wondering where our next meal is coming from. Pretty darn good, don't you think?"

He obviously expected her to be happy, but she

was confused.

"Of course, it's wonderful, and I'm very happy for you, but where did the money come from? I don't know anything about any bridge financing. I mean, I know what bridge financing is, but no one has mentioned it in relation to this project. It didn't just fall out of the sky."

He shrugged his shoulders and turned up both palms. "Hey, I don't look a gift horse in the mouth. The equipment arrived and deposits were made to our bank accounts, so we're happy campers. Maybe God just loves us because we're working so hard for a good cause."

He grinned and did a little jig. "Whaddya say, Paula? Aren't we lucky?"

She snorted softly, then took out her cell phone and dialed the Chemistry Department office. Lottie answered on the first ring. "Lottie, it's Paula. Look, I'm in Sam's lab, and Barry is showing me the upgrades that were made with what he calls bridge financing."

"Yes," Lottie interrupted. "Isn't it wonderful? It's not a lot, but it'll give them some peace of mind until the big companies come through. We're just thrilled."

"But where did that money come from, and why wasn't I advised? I'm tracking the kids' hours to make sure they're paid appropriately, and I'm keeping records of all purchases. I didn't know anything about this."

"Oh, dear," Lottie soothed. "I'm sure I don't know. All I had was delivery receipts for the things that went into the lab, and they're all marked *Paid in Full*. I gave them all to Barry. But everything seems to be in order, so I wouldn't worry."

"Yes, I understand, but who paid for them?" Paula insisted. "That's my question. And who deposited money to the students' bank accounts? This is not correct protocol, and I'm worried. This is no way to conduct business."

Lottie was quiet for a moment, then Paula heard her sigh.

"I guess the only one who could tell you that would be Professor Mackenzie. He's the money man, you know."

Of course. Boyd Mackenzie. "Okay. Do you know if he's in his office today?"

"Just a minute, let me check his schedule." A pause. "Oh, yes, he's here until three o'clock. He's in two-twelve, upstairs and down the hall. Shall I tell him you're on your way?"

But Paula had already hung up. She put the delivery receipts in her briefcase and took the stairs at a trot. At the door of office 212, she threw her shoulders back, straightened her spine, and rapped sharply on the door.

Boyd opened the door to an intriguing picture before him. Her copper curls were in disarray, and one had slipped low over an angry green eye. A soft beige sweater topped formfitting tan slacks, and high-heeled boots brought her flushed face to the level of his chin.

"Mrs. Wincott," he acknowledged, his voice only a little hoarse. "Do come in. Are you here as a chemistry student, or is this a social visit?" He gestured to a seat directly in front of his desk.

Taking in the totality of the room, she didn't move. Tidy yet definitely lived in. The furniture was standard university issue, but somehow he had managed to personalize it with a few pieces of art on the walls. A coffeemaker and mismatched mugs rested on top of a small refrigerator. Deep-pile carpet covered the floor; an over-sized leather chair sat at the studded oak desk. The most unsettling feature was Boyd himself.

Wearing faded brown cords and a navy blue sweater with the sleeves pushed up, he looked decidedly unlike a college professor except for the reading glasses sitting on the bridge of his nose, his only concession to middle age. For the first time she noticed crinkles at his eyes and a single crease above his brow which only added to his appeal. She caught the heady scent of his skin and felt a tiny skittering along her nerves. The moment hung while each assessed the charge in the air.

He took a step backwards and again invited her into the room. This time she crossed to the chair he indicated and seated herself stiffly. "I'm here in my capacity as lab project coordinator. I have a few questions."

He eased his long frame into the leather chair opposite her and leaned back. "What can I do for you, Ms. Lab Project Coordinator?"

Ignoring his smug look, she removed the delivery receipts from her briefcase and spread them out on the desk. "I've just been to the lab where Barry showed me new instruments and several pieces of brand-new equipment. He tells me they've been paid some of their back salary—by direct deposit. No paper checks were written; the money just showed up in their accounts." She leaned forward to make her point with an narrowed, unwavering gaze.

His expression remained unchanged. Finally he replied, "Yes, that's true. And what exactly is your question, Mrs. Wincott?" The extra stress put on her formal name only irritated her further.

She gave him the *are you an idiot* look that Emma had so often given her, then started firing questions. "Where did the money come from? How did it get into the kids' bank accounts? Who paid for the equipment?" She delivered the last with clearly evident irritation. "And why wasn't I kept in the loop?"

Boyd slowly steepled his fingers and rested his

chin on them. "Well, now, I believe I can set your inquiring mind at rest. The money came from local sources, contacts that have a strong community spirit. It was deposited directly from those sources. The equipment was donated, and I didn't think it was important enough to involve you at this level. I thought we were working together on the large sum funding. This is just odds and ends, bits and pieces."

Unsatisfied, her voice rose, her eyes sparked. "That's not your decision to make, Professor. I'm in charge of everything except the grant applications, and you have deliberately gone ahead without consulting me. You've undermined my authority and made me look as if I don't know what's going on in my own husband's lab."

He leaned forward with a furrowed brow and spoke very softly. "Are you suggesting, Mrs. Wincott, that we should be working together more closely?"

Stung, she opened her mouth, but he didn't wait for her answer. "Why, every time I try to take a moment to discuss anything with you, I'm met with withering glances and stone-faced refusals. For reasons you have yet to explain, you've been nothing but stubborn and ungracious, unreasonably irritable, and you've exhibited the emotional maturity of a three-year-old in a temper tantrum. Why would I want to put myself through that unless it's absolutely necessary?"

He held her eyes with an unfathomable gaze while she tried to keep her emotions on an even keel. He was baiting her, and she bit the hook.

Control broken, she pounded the desk with her palm. "You blame me for this? Well, you're right, I don't want to work with you, I don't want to see you, I don't want to know you. And if you had never come here, I wouldn't be in this position. Sam would still be running his own lab, and everything would be just as it was."

"Is that so?"

She took a quick breath and forged ahead. "Sam was a genius. Everyone knew it. Did you know he published a ground-breaking paper on direct methods for the determination of crystal structures when he was only twenty-five years old?"

He nodded, perhaps to slow her down, but she was on a roll.

He was the idol of every student who ever knew him—until you waltzed in from who knows where. Hmph, you're not even an American!"

"A minor point, irrelevant."

"The point, in case you've missed it," she all but shouted, "is that you stole his thunder. You became the center of attention, the focus of the department, the wunderkind who took his place."

"Not true." He spoke firmly but without matching her decibel level.

"Oh, no? There are more sections of biochemistry and fewer sections of inorganic, and more money comes to the school from the NIH than from all of Sam's sources combined. How do you think that made him feel?"

She answered her own question. "He hated you! How could you think I would want anything to do with you?"

Caught up in her tirade, she was unaware that he had risen until he rounded the desk and lifted her from her chair. He held her tightly against his chest, her hands pinned against him. Her breath fanned his face. She felt the rapid beat of his heart beneath her hands, and was startled to note the matching thump of her own heart. He stared into her flushed face for a long moment. His gaze lingered on her for a moment, then he spoke decisively yet quietly.

"That will be enough. You may not speak to me in that tone, and you may not make wildly foolish accusations that I somehow caused an injury to a colleague."

She dared not move while he continued in a tight voice. "Sam was a colleague, a colleague who had and still has my respect as a man and as a scientist. If he hated me, he never betrayed it to me. There was no reason for us to be competitors. I came here because Ed King made me a generous offer, and I tried to do my job to the best of my ability. I don't have a guru complex, nor do I seek out undue attention. It's true I have a knack for finding money, but I've never known that to be a sin."

He loosened his grip but did not release her. She hoped he didn't feel her tremble. "Now, we can do this the easy way, as two collaborators with a common goal, or we can do it the hard way, as two enemies forced to work together on an onerous task. But I have made a commitment to this project, and we *will* work together."

He relinquished his hold so suddenly that she stumbled backwards. He placed the receipts back into her bag and handed it to her. Without another word, he guided her toward the door and opened it. "It's your decision. I can work either way."

He ushered her through the door and shut it firmly behind her. Outside she leaned her back against the wall and to gather her composure. Her throat hurt with the effort not to cry. Nothing was working out right.

****

On the other side of the door, Boyd pulled himself together. Her passionate outburst had pushed him to an angry response that he now regretted. But she touched something inside him, and he had been so close to kissing her he could almost feel her on his tongue. And what a mistake that would have been. He congratulated himself for steering clear of dangerous waters. But he couldn't help but wonder how she would have tasted.

CHAPTER EIGHT

Early Saturday morning, Paula pulled up outside Emma's house to find the front door open, with Ben and Chloe, both dressed in sweatshirts and jeans, waiting. When they saw her, they let out screeches and raced toward the car. Emma appeared in the doorway to wave good-bye.

"We'll be back when we get back," Paula shouted. "Don't expect us anytime soon."

Firmly strapped in, Ben and Chloe sat in the back seat with the picnic basket between them, chattering about nothing in particular, and Paula was content just to be with them. She loved their outings to the canyons, and she always prepared an enormous lunch to accommodate their amazing appetites.

She glanced at them in the rear-view mirror, noting their differences yet seeing herself and Sam in both of them. Ben had insisted his sandy brown hair be buzz cut, and the sun had faded the ends to a taffy blond. Except for his hair, he resembled the young Sam more and more. Chloe's four-year old face was all cherub, but she had inherited Paula's bright hair. Too soon she would come to hate those curls when she found them impossible to tame. She had already complained that she didn't like her *pink* hair.

"Nana," Ben's voice broke her reverie. "How come Grandpa never took us on picnics? Didn't he like us?"

She was startled by the question but quick to defend Sam.

"Of course he liked you, sweetheart. He loved you and Chloe very much. You were his special little munchkins."

"Then why didn't he do stuff with us?"

"You know Grandpa was a very busy man, a scientist who worked very hard. He just didn't have time," she finished, wishing she had a better answer and hoping the boy understood.

"I guess so," he sighed. "Mom says he was the smartest man in the whole world."

"That's right. Your grandpa was the smartest man in the whole world."

She parked the car at the bottom of Bluebell Canyon and gathered up a blanket and the basket of food. The climb into the canyon was not arduous, but it was a steady incline. After thirty minutes, she was ready to deposit the picnic hamper and take a breather. Ben and Chloe had run ahead, and Paula had to call them back with the lure of food.

They spread the thick red blanket in the cool shade of a stand of cottonwood trees, and the children immediately fell upon the hamper.

"Nana, may we open the basket now?" Ben pleaded.

These days he seemed to be always hungry, packing man-sized meals into his wiry body, tanned from the long summer, and muscular, even for a six-year old.

"Please, Nana, I stahvving." Chloe turned bright blue eyes and an irresistible face to her and the basket. Fried chicken, potato salad, baked beans, coleslaw, carrot sticks, and home-made biscuits filled every nook, but Paula took out only one drumstick for each child.

"Why don't we eat a piece of chicken while we pick a big bouquet of wildflowers to put on our picnic blanket. It'll make our lunch look special, don't you think?"

She passed out the finger foods to take the edge of their appetites, then shed her pullover sweater and dropped it on the blanket. "Let's see who can find the prettiest flowers," she challenged, setting off at a leisurely pace with the children running ahead to pick the blossoms growing alongside the well-worn path into the canyon.

She glanced up toward the Flatirons and saw a number of tiny spots scattered here and there: free climbers pitting themselves against sheer rock. She shook her head at the foolishness and unnecessary danger of rock climbing. Young people and their inexplicable behavior. She devoutly hoped Ben wouldn't grow into such a daring young man. Of course, level-headed Emma and Wesley would make sure of that.

When she was a student many years ago, the vast initials CU had once been lovingly carved into the mountainside. It was a symbol of another time, her youth, and she felt a tug of melancholy at its loss. As her eye moved to the former site of the vanished icon, she caught a glimpse of one young man in particular who was moving doggedly toward the top with rope and harness slung over his shoulder. He hung by one arm as he scrabbled for a foothold and swung himself outward and upward. Even as far away as he was, she could see he was bare-chested, wearing only dark climbing pants and shoes. She shuddered when he slipped momentarily, dangling precariously while he reached for a handhold. She closed her eyes for an instant, then looked again to see if he was still there. He had caught a grip and was continuing his crab-like climb up the face of the rock.

She had seen enough.

She turned back to the path and caught up to the children. The sun was warm on her back, and the flowers were brilliant in yellows, reds, and, of course, the blue of the bluebells. It was Indian summer, and Boulder was enchanting. As she had done many times before, she thought how lucky she was and how much she had to be thankful for. As long as the sun kissed her face and she had such a fine family, she should be, and could be, content with her life.

Several bouquets later, Ben and Chloe raced her back to the blanket and dived again for the picnic basket. Ben opened the lid and looked eagerly to Paula. "It's time, Nana, okay? I can take everything out. Chloe, what do you want?"

He pulled out plates and spoons and reached for the homemade brownies Paula had hidden in the very bottom of the basket.

She placed the flowers in the middle of the blanket and arranged them like a centerpiece. She dished up chicken, potato salad, and baked beans for each child, taking care to include carrot sticks for Chloe. From the tiny beads of perspiration on their upper lips, she could see they were ready for a cool drink. She poured cold lemonade from a thermos and settled each child with a sturdy cup.

As she sat back against the trunk of a tree with her plate, Paula knew a moment of peace. Sam had never shown an interest in picnicking with children, his own or his grandchildren, so it was a relatively new experience for her, one she wanted to cultivate with regularity. Morgan and Emma had grown up far too fast; only a split second passed before they were adults. She felt as if she had a second chance with the grandchildren, a chance to enjoy every childhood moment with them. Serenity filled her.

The food and the sun worked their magic, and, with a full stomach, Chloe laid her head in Paula's lap and fell asleep. Ben was more interested in gathering rocks, but he was careful not to wander too far away from the blanket. Paula leaned back against the tree, and, without realizing it, slowly drifted off into deep delicious sleep. She dreamed of color and movement but nothing definite, just contentment.

"Hey, buddy, whatcha got there?"

From a distance, she heard a male voice but couldn't pull herself out of the honeyed depths of languorous afternoon sleep.

"Rocks," Ben replied. "I collect rocks, and these are good ones. Wanta see?"

She started awake and looked up. A man was talking to Ben. Because he was back lit by the sun, she couldn't make out features. But that voice was familiar. The man knelt beside Ben to examine the rocks he held in his little-boy hands. "Those are first-rate, I'd say. This must be a good place to hunt."

"You bet it is," Ben said vigorously. "My Nana brings me up here a lot so I get all different kinds. I even found some purple ones last time."

"Your Nana?"

Ben pointed. "Yeah, that's her over there, sleeping. We had a picnic."

Embarrassed at having been caught napping, Paula slid Chloe's head off her lap and got to her feet. When she did so, she realized Ben was talking to the rock climber.

And the rock climber was Boyd Mackenzie!

He turned to her with an innocuous smile. Inexplicably, her heart tripped over itself.

"Well, hello, Nana. This is quite a grandson you have here, and he's gathered some fine rocks." He turned back to Ben. "What's your name, son?"

"My name is Ben, and that's my sister. She's sleeping 'cuz she's still a baby." Ben pointed to the unconscious Chloe. "Her name's Chloe."

Boyd examined the rocks Ben held out to him. "I collect rocks too, and I always gather a few every time I come up here." He handed the rocks back to

Ben. "Want to see what I found today?"

"You betcha." Ben pocketed his rocks and moved closer to Boyd.

Boyd reached into his back pocket and drew out six tiny, perfectly-formed pieces of granite. Some were pink, some a faint purple, and one had gold streaks running through it.

Ben whistled. "Wow, Mister, those are super! I bet you have to climb up pretty high to find those, don't you?"

Boyd chuckled. "Yes sir, you surely do have to climb up high, and that's a fact."

Paula took in the sight of the bare-chested Boyd Mackenzie, tan and fit, gloves covered in chalk, rope wrapped around his body, blue pants torn, and black climbing shoes scuffed from frequent battles with the rock. His hair was mussed, his face sweat streaked. She hated to admit it, but he looked magnificent.

She swallowed before she spoke. "Ben, I'm sure this nice man has things to do, so let's not keep him," she began. "Say good-bye now."

Boyd looked her full in the face, and without changing expression he replied, "Actually, I don't have anything to do. I came down from my climb because I was getting really hungry."

He looked pointedly at the spread of food on the blanket, then he smiled at Ben.

Ben took the hint. "Oh, Nana, we have lots of food. He can have some of ours, can't he?" He ran to the blanket and began digging through potato salad and chicken. "Nana, you can give him some lemonade. And there's lots of potato salad and beans left." He tilted his head and confided to Boyd, "And my Nana makes the best brownies in the whole world."

Faced with a fait accompli, Paula had no choice. Gritting her teeth, she agreed. "Sure, Ben, he can have some of our picnic." She turned to Boyd, "I think we still have plenty of everything. What would you like?"

He rose slowly and looked at her steadily. "Everything."

Heat suffused her neck and face, and her gaze failed. He removed his climbing gloves, slapped them against his thigh to remove chalk, then stuffed them into his back pocket. With the rope still criss-crossed around his bare torso, he looked nothing like a university professor. He was an animal pitting himself against the elements, courting the danger of the Flatirons. Perspiration glistened on his shoulders and ran down through the thick hairs on his chest. Scratches mixed with chalk in half a dozen places. His blatant sensuality both frightened and attracted.

With unsteady hands, she filled a plate and handed him a cup of lemonade. Their hands brushed together when he accepted the plate, and her breath caught in her throat. His lips turned up slightly, and she realized he had heard and understood.

"Thank you," he murmured, almost secretly, and, without another word, he settled himself cross-legged on a corner of the blanket, Ben close beside him. She suddenly felt a tiny chill. She picked up her pullover and tugged it over her head.

To her chagrin, Ben seemed taken with Boyd. He nudged closer to Boyd's side and asked "Did you climb up to the top?"

"Yep," Boyd replied between bites of chicken. "I climbed up, then across, and down again. Didn't you see me up there?"

He stole a quick look at Paula, but her face revealed nothing.

Ben's eyes were saucers. "Boy, that must be lots of fun. Do you think I could do that when I get bigger? Mom says I'm growing really fast, and I'm already strong. Then I could find those special rocks like you do."

"I don't know about that. I guess you'd have to ask your parents about learning to climb. It's really hard work, and you can get hurt."

Boyd caught Paula's eye and held out his cup for more lemonade. "You'd have to grow a lot bigger and practice a long time before you could climb the Flatirons."

Hoping to distract Ben from his conversation with Boyd and, at the same time, urging Boyd to hurry along, she poured another drink. "Who else would like more lemonade?"

"Me, Nana!"

Chloe rolled over and sat up. She rubbed the sleep from her eyes and took in the newcomer without expression. "I want more drink."

But Ben was not to be deterred. He placed an eager hand on Boyd's forearm. "Do you like kids?"

Boyd smiled down at him. "I like them very much."

"Do you gots any?"

Boyd looked at Chloe, just finishing off her cup of lemonade, red-gold hair tousled from sleep, and shook his head.

"No, I'm very sorry to say I don't. But right now I really wish I did. I teach at the university, and I used to know your grandpa, so I've heard all about you and your sister. He was very proud of you both."

"You knew my grandpa? Well, maybe you could visit us sometime," Ben urged. "Couldn't he, Nana? We don't live very far, and my mom wouldn't mind. She likes it when people come to visit. Isn't that right, Nana?"

Boyd had painted himself into a corner. He turned to Paula with a helpless gesture. She stood up and began gathering up the remnants of the picnic. "I'm sure this nice gentleman has lots of things to do, Ben, so we shouldn't take up any more of his time today. Say good-bye, and help me clean up."

Boyd took his cue and stood. He threw the chicken scraps into the plastic bag she held out to him and wiped his hands on his pants. He leaned toward her and offered a soft conciliation.

"Don't worry, Paula, I won't take him up on his offer. But he's a nice kid."

He was standing so close she could see the sweat on his chest, and she caught the erotic scent of male musk. "You're very lucky to have a couple of fine grandchildren."

He backed away a few feet and waved good-bye to Ben. "It was very nice to meet you. Thanks for the lunch and the pleasant company. Maybe I'll see you again sometime." He turned and started down the path.

"Wait, mister," yelled Ben. "What's your name?

Boyd looked over one shoulder and threw a warm smile. "My name is Boyd. Your Nana knows who I am."

Then he raised his arm in the air and waved it once again before disappearing into the brush below them.

****

Farther down the path, Boyd realized he had called her Paula. His use of her Christian name was somehow intimate, almost as if he had physically touched her. It had slipped out naturally. And she hadn't bristled or corrected him. He began to whistle.

As he walked, he contemplated the serendipity that had thrown them together. When he had spied her sleeping under the tree, his visceral reaction had jolted him. In repose, her face free of bitterness and suspicion, she was ravishing. Her skin, unmarred by wrinkles, was ivory touched with gold. She had tiny laugh lines around her eyes that he had never seen before and which he found exceptionally attractive. Her lips were full and faintly touched with what appeared to be natural rose. He understood why Sam Wincott had kept this long-limbed beauty to himself.

CHAPTER NINE

For the next few weeks, Paula stayed under the radar. She didn't want to run into Boyd until she had come to terms with her ambivalent feelings about the developing relationship. She was grateful to be free of his class. It would have been a mistake to interact with him in the role of student to teacher three times a week.

The mishmash of papers in the lab cubicle slowly turned into well-organized loose-leaf notebooks, arranged in chronological order so the student scientists could retrieve notes in a moment. She was able to persuade them to file their work at the end of each session rather than simply leaving it on the desk for her to compile later. Much to her satisfaction, Sam's old style of efficiency slowly crept back. Then, to her surprise, the students appeared to respect her and enjoy her visits. Without trying, she had developed a rapport with them that went beyond her routine tasks. They shared personal conversations, even talked about their goals and aspirations. It was like having a very large family of like-minded folks, and she loved it.

As Thanksgiving fast approached, Emma decided to make the dinner at her house. "It would be good for you, Mom. You've made Thanksgiving dinner every year of my life. It's about time I took over that chore and let you relax. I promise I'll check with you before trying anything difficult."

After considering for a long moment, Paula acquiesced, acknowledging that while another chapter in her life had closed, perhaps a new one was beginning. "If you're sure you want to do all of that cooking. But you have to let me bring the pies," she insisted. "And, since I'm the only one who eats them, I'll bring those tasty celery sticks with cream cheese and pineapple."

Emma moaned. "Ugh. I don't know why you like those things, but okay. We'll eat about three, so come early. Wes will have hot apple cider ready."

"Sounds great."

"And, Mom, plan to stay late. I've got a great DVD of *Sense and Sensibility*. Since Wes and the kids always fall asleep after dinner, you and I can watch it together."

"I'd like that, sweetheart. I'll be there around two. And I'll be ready for that hot apple cider. If there's anything else you need, just give me a call."

When she arrived home on the Wednesday before Thanksgiving, she found a message from Ed King on the answering machine, reminding her of the dinner dance on Saturday night. She had agreed to act as one of the chaperones, an archaic term, and it had slipped her mind. For a woman who had been at loose ends, she now had a full plate, and was actually enjoying it! Every day was a new adventure.

She stopped at the grocery store for all of the pie makings and planned to spend the evening creating her specialties—cherry, peach, and pumpkin. It was overkill, but Emma favored cherry, Wesley was a fan of peach, and Chloe and Ben demanded pumpkin. The truth was that baking for her loved ones relaxed and comforted her, reminding her of the early days when she cooked for a growing family.

Back then, her days were filled with cooking and sewing, taking meticulous care of all aspects of family life. She made all of Emma's clothes, played den mother for both Morgan and Emma's scouting activities, was a devoted PTA member, and volunteered for any and all activities involving the children. Sam had expected a hundred percent. She happily gave it.

After a quick grilled-cheese sandwich, she poured herself a glass of sherry, put on an apron over jeans and CU sweatshirt, and laid out the supplies. She was elbow deep in flour and pie crust when the telephone rang so she let the answering machine pick it up.

"Paula, it's Boyd. I'm about a block from your house and thought I'd stop in for a moment to have you look over the final grant application before I send it off. I don't want to start another fracas by doing anything behind your back or by not consulting you, so I'll be there in a couple of minutes."

No, no, no. She scrambled for the telephone, but he hung up before she could reach it and tell him not to come.

She was trying to think of escape when she heard the doorbell ring. With house lights on and her car in the driveway, he would know she was home. She threw off the apron and ran a hand through her hair. With her stomach turning flip-flops, there was nothing else to do but answer the doorbell.

She opened the door to a wave of cold air and Boyd, the essence of male in a sheepskin jacket with a blue muffler looped around his neck, standing on the stoop. The tip of his nose was red from the cold, and she could see his breath in the early evening air. She stood still, taking in the full effect of the picture before her.

"Sorry to bother you, but I'll just take a minute." He carried a sheaf of papers in his hands and waved them in the air.

"I'm actually on my way out for the evening, but I wanted to get this out of the way, if you don't mind."

She backed into the room and pointed in the

direction of the kitchen. As she closed the living room door, she looked through the glass pane. His car, the *flashy sports car* she thought inappropriate for a man of his years, was parked in front of her house. What would the neighbors think?

And what was that in the front seat? She barely made out a female figure seated in the passenger seat. In the fading light of early evening she discerned pale blonde hair and what appeared to be a fur jacket. He had a date. With someone wearing animal pelts.

Spine tight, she found herself unreasonably on edge. She followed him to the kitchen where he had already seated himself at the table and had loosened his muffler. His hair, ruffled by the windy evening, only added to his appeal. She was suddenly aware of the flour on her hands, possibly on her face, and the mundane surroundings. He looked confident and completely at ease while she, recalling the blonde waiting in the car, felt miserably inadequate.

He inhaled deeply then exhaled loudly. "Ahhh, smells good in here. Are you making Thanksgiving for your family?"

"Just a few pies," she replied shortly. "My daughter is hosting dinner at her house this year."

Having him sit so comfortably in her kitchen made her feel vulnerable at a time when she needed strong defenses against those unnerving gold specks in the depths of his blue eyes.

"Your daughter. Is that the mother of those two beautiful children I met at Bluebell Canyon?"

Paula didn't answer.

"Look, I want to thank you for smoothing over a difficult situation. I didn't mean to intrude on you and your family. I didn't realize the boy was with you when I first saw him on the trail, and, well, he's such a cute little fellow. He's got a great personality."

She wiped her hands on a dish towel and sat opposite him. She felt jittery, and she didn't like it. "Since you have plans for the evening, just show me what you brought so you can get on with your date, okay?

He raised one hand, palm out. "Whoa. No need to get testy. I'm not in a hurry and wanted to make sure we're in sync. There's a lot of technical verbiage to go through, which probably won't make any sense to you. The important thing is that I not submit these proposals without your knowledge and approval." He gave her a pointed look. "Isn't that right?"

He was being completely reasonable, and she felt silly making such a big fuss, but the blonde in the fur jacket niggled at her brain. She ground her teeth but said nothing. What could she say? His private life was his own.

He began pulling papers from the manila envelope. "Didn't we decide we would work closely together?"

He lingered over the word *closely* just enough to catch her attention. His eyes were smoky, almost sleepy, and Paula felt light headed but still made no response. Her tongue felt thick, and she couldn't formulate a clear thought.

She cleared a place for the papers, and he laid them out for her. Then he moved to the chair beside her and scrunched himself close to her. He angled the papers so they both could read at the same time. His proximity made her nervous, but she made no move to elude him. She needed to get through the application if only to get him out of her house.

Let the furry blonde have him.

"The first few pages are merely an introduction," he began, "just to give an overview of the project and to list Sam's credentials. You can read through them fairly quickly."

Paula read the first page, but she wasn't able to absorb any of it. She read each line over again, but Boyd's nearness stirred her senses, and she found herself simply staring at the page. He leaned in to point out several important paragraphs. He read the significant parts aloud, making sure she understood them. She nodded absently and uh-hummed at most of them.

Without her realizing it, he placed one arm on the back of her chair and moved so close their knees touched. She felt the warmth of his body but didn't move and hoped he didn't notice. She didn't know how long they had sat there or how many pages he read to her. She was afraid to move for fear he would become aware of her as well as the tension in the air.

"This is really the meat and potatoes of the application. I'm quite proud of the final draft, and believe we stand a good chance for a substantial grant. Sam's work is groundbreaking."

As he continued reading, she felt his breath on her cheek and smelled the fresh autumn outdoors on his jacket. She heard rushing sounds in her ears and felt a jab of what could only be fear. She wanted to flee but could find no logical reason. She looked up, intending to ask him to move his chair, but she found her face only inches from his, so close his breath warmed her cheek. His presence immobilized her, and his mouth... his mouth.

Boyd appeared deeply engrossed in the task at hand and unaware of the thickness in the air. But now she was so close she could see the pulse beating at the base of his neck. Suddenly his hand paused in its progress across the page, and he choked on the words he was reading. He turned a puzzled face to her, and they stared at each other for an interminable moment—neither one able to interpret the tension. She felt like a rabbit caught in headlights. His gaze told her he found it irresistible.

So he didn't try to resist, simply tilted his head, and found her throat with his lips.

Helpless, drunk with desire, she allowed her head to fall back against his arm, granting him increased access as a tiny cry escaped her lips. He traced the line of her neck with his lips, nuzzling softly. While one arm tightened around her shoulders, the other hand touched her cheek. His mouth found hers open and waiting. He enveloped her, invaded her, devoured her—and she was unable to protest. The kiss went on and on until she felt faint, but still it didn't end. Their breath mingled, he captured her tongue and sucked gently, and something akin to warm molasses ran through her body until she became languid and liquid. He tasted delicious, and she wanted to go on tasting him. Without conscious awareness, her arm slipped around his neck and held him while she met his kiss and returned it equally, whimpering in the back of her throat when his hand found her breast.

Abruptly, he released her and rose unsteadily, holding the edge of the table for balance. He ran a hand across his face and stared at her uncomprehendingly. The moment stretched like a taut bowstring, humming with suppressed energy.

"Paula," was all he said, his voice strained and hoarse. "I'm—"

He looked at her curiously, then gathered up his papers and turned to leave. She watched him walk unevenly to the front door, open it, then turn back.

"Paula, I—" He faltered again, shook his head as if to clear it, then turned and closed the door behind him.

She waited for the shame to run through her, but, to her surprise and confusion, it failed to appear. She felt vitally alive, exhilarated, and completely disoriented. She could still savor him on her tongue, and the droning continued in her ears.

A long time later, she gathered herself enough to finish the baking and take a long hot bath. She sat with a washcloth over her face, drifting, reliving that moment with Boyd, trying to explore her behavior, her feelings. It wasn't until she entered the bedroom she had shared with Sam that the sense of betrayal hit her—hard.

She had allowed—no, encouraged another man to make advances to her, and in Sam's house. That it was Boyd Mackenzie made her betrayal more reprehensible. Deep shame flooded her heart, and she wept cold tears.

CHAPTER TEN

Thanksgiving dinner with the family restored Paula's equanimity. She arrived early to find Emma's house in its usual state of chaos, but the noise and clutter soothed her and reminded her who she was.

Wesley's hot cider was perfect, and, as he handed her a cinnamon stick for stirring, he bantered, "You're looking particularly attractive today, my girl. School seems to agree with you. You're positively radiant."

She stepped over Ben's train set that ran through the middle of the living room and found her way to the sofa. "Well," she sighed, sinking into the battered cushions, "I've been pleasantly surprised, I must say. I thought I'd have a hard time, being so much older than the other students, I mean. I thought they would be so much brighter than I am. But it's all coming back to me, and I'm really enjoying my studies."

"It shows. There's an energy I haven't seen in a long time. It's very becoming."

"Thank you, my love," she allowed. "I'm feeling alive again. I thought I had died along with Sam, but every day brings something new, and I'm feeling better as time goes on."

Mischief lit up his warm brown eyes and made his face positively handsome. "So, what's this I hear about a certain rock climber? Care to share with your son-in-law, or do I have to get all of my information from Ben?"

She almost spilled her cider. "What? I'm... not

sure what you mean." She set the cup on the coffee table and fingered the double strand of pearls at her throat and, unsure of how much he already knew, stalled. "A rock climber, you say?"

She knew full well that Ben must have mentioned Boyd to his parents, but she wasn't going to make it easy for Wesley. Her heart was thudding, but she kept a serene face.

He settled himself beside her and continued a bit too casually, "Oh, nothing important, I'm sure. Ben just told us you ran into a rock-climbing acquaintance of yours. He said the fellow knew you and that you gave him fried chicken." Wesley's eyebrows rose as he added, "He also said he was a really *old* fellow, like a granddad. Are you holding out on us?"

"Oh, that." She tried to sound dismissive. She tugged at the bottom of her new yellow sweater and smoothed her skirt, playing for time. "When we were picnicking in Bluebell Canyon, we bumped into a former colleague of Sam's, a biochemist, I believe he said. They didn't know each other well, but he did mention that he teaches at the university."

She paused to take a sip of cider while Wesley waited. "He had some rocks that impressed Ben, so we chatted for a moment. That's all. I don't know where Ben got the impression that we knew each other."

"You gave him fried chicken," he prompted with a sly grin.

She shrugged. "Well, yes. He said he was hungry, and well, you know our Ben. He insisted we had to feed him. I gave him a piece of chicken and sent him on his way. It was nothing at all. Really."

He pushed. "Ben said this fellow talked nice to you and said you knew him. He said you gave him lemonade."

"Well, it was a hot day, and he asked for

lemonade." She smiled to take the edge off the sharpness in her voice. "Really, Wes, it was nothing."

"Are you guys talking about that Boyd man?"

Ben suddenly ran through the room, wearing a Spiderman outfit and literally yelling his question. He stopped only momentarily to direct his comments to Paula. "I like him, Nana. When can he come to visit?" With that, Spiderman continued his flight through the living room and into the kitchen.

Wesley gave Paula a knowing look. "Boyd? You don't mean Hamish Boyd, the Anthropology professor? He's not so old, but I guess to Ben he'd seem like an old guy."

Pointedly ignoring him, she called to Emma, "Honey, shall I come and help you?"

Before Emma had a chance to reply, Paula picked up her cider and smiled at Wesley. "I'd better see how she's doing. The first time you make Thanksgiving dinner can be overwhelming. Good cider, Wes."

He chuckled and let her go. "So, that's all I get, eh?" He smiled and saluted her with his cup.

She blew him a kiss, then exited the room without looking back. She counted herself lucky at a narrow escape.

Between the two of them, Paula and Emma produced an exceptionally fine dinner, replete with the buttery biscuits Paula had taught Emma to make when she was a little girl. They had always been a huge favorite, and Emma took pride in making them just perfect. When Chloe was big enough, the three of them would make biscuits together, and the tradition would be passed on to another generation. Just looking at the biscuits warmed Paula's heart. It was the little things that made life such a joy.

Between helpings of turkey and cranberry sauce, she avoided any conversation that might lead to questions about the rock climber. Emma asked about the progress in the lab, and Paula was delighted to tell her how well it was going. She mentioned the interim financing, but she was careful not to reveal who arranged it, and no one asked.

"So, Mom, are you finding it too much?"

Not surprised at Emma's directness, Paula had a ready answer. "Not at all. You may be surprised to know I'm actually invigorated by all of the responsibilities. I'm taking only one class, and it's turned out to be a lot less hazardous than I had anticipated. It's World Lit, and it's proving to be exciting. I'll add chemistry next term, and I'm sure I'll be able to muddle through."

She put down her knife and fork and folded her hands under her chin. She leaned toward Emma. "The best part is I'm tidying up the mess in your dad's lab and can see his work living on in his students. I can't explain to you how much that means to me. It's more than just having something to fill my day. I have people who need and rely on me. I can make a difference."

Before Emma could respond, Wesley poured another splash of white wine into her glass and took the conversation in a new direction. "And don't forget you get to go to the Chemistry Department parties. Who's taking you to the one on Saturday?"

His expression was bland, but Paula caught the undercurrent.

She shook her finger at him and narrowed her eyes in what she hoped was a warning look. "No one is taking me to the dinner dance, Mr. Smarty, and you know that. I'm going alone, and I'll be sitting with Ed and Helen King and the rest of the old folks, trying to maintain some semblance of decorum amongst those wild hellions they call students."

He choked on his laughter and held up his hands. "Okay, okay, I was just asking. I thought maybe your rock climber might be in the picture somewhere."

Emma pierced Paula with a look. "What rock climber?" She turned to Wesley, "What are you talking about?"

"Mom, Mom, may I be excused?" Ben was already out of his chair and racing outside.

Chloe fidgeted in her chair. "Me too, Mommy? Please me ascuse?"

Emma waved them away. "Okay, Sweetheart. Go out and play, but don't leave the yard, and be careful not to let Abner out. I'll call you when we cut the pies."

She turned her attention back to Paula with renewed determination. "What is Wes talking about, Mom?"

Paula gave him a killer look, but his expression was innocent. "Oh, it's nothing, darling. Wes is just being silly. Aren't you, Wesley?"

With a look of defeat, he surrendered. "Yes, ladies, I'm just being silly. I know there's no one in your life, Paula. More's the pity."

But Emma wasn't so easily appeased. "Don't make that kind of a joke," she rebuked. "Of course there's no one in her life. My mother is a respectable widow, a middle-aged widow at that, and she's certainly not interested in some rock climber."

He shrugged, but Emma hung on. "No, really, I can't believe you would say that even in jest. Mom was devoted to Dad. They had a perfect, once-in-a-lifetime marriage, and she has dedicated herself to perpetuating his memory through his work."

But he wasn't listening. He was already at sideboard, vigorously cutting into the pies. Brandishing a silver pie cutter, he turned to the ladies. "Who wants peach?"

CHAPTER ELEVEN

When Saturday's skies turned clear with a brisk wind, Paula found herself looking forward to the evening's festivities. She was genuinely fond of Ed King and his wife, Helen, a former cheerleader whose bubbly personality had matured into cheery good humor. She was the perfect foil for Ed's sober scientific demeanor, and they made a handsome couple. Paula was in good spirits as she went through her wardrobe to select a dress that would strike just the right note of formality and maturity. Black, she thought, would be appropriate for her age and position in the community.

On her way to the kitchen for a quick lunch, she noticed the light blinking on the answering machine. She hadn't heard the telephone ring, but someone had left a message. Thinking it might be from Ed or Emma, she depressed the Play button.

"*Paula.*"

She froze.

"*It's Boyd.*"

A long pause followed, then, "*I want to... uh... apologize for... well, you know.*" She heard him take a long, shaky breath before his words picked up some steam. "*It was entirely my fault. I don't know what came over me. Well, actually I do know, but that's neither here nor there.*"

Another long pause. She heard uneasy breathing. "*Anyway, I don't want you to be afraid of me. I mean, afraid to see me, afraid it might happen again. I find you very attractive, but I also respect you as Sam's widow... And... oh, God, Paula, I'm just trying to say I'm sorry."*

She snapped off the machine. Why did he find it necessary to bring it up again? She preferred to forget the incident altogether and get on with her life.

There was no real need to see him again. The grant apps were submitted. All they had to do now was wait. Could she believe the sincerity of his apology? If he felt so bad, why had he waited three days to call? Why did he call on the very day when he knew she might run into him again? No, he was trying to manipulate the situation to his own advantage. But to what end?

She would cancel. She could plead illness or something—anything to avoid his company. Ed King would undoubtedly seat him at the King table, and she would be unable to avoid him.

She picked up the telephone and dialed Ed's home number.

"Hello, King residence," Helen answered in her usual jovial manner.

"Helen, it's Paula."

"Oh, Paula, I'm so happy you called. I can't tell you how much I'm looking forward to seeing you tonight. I'm so sorry I missed the last faculty dance. I'm sure Ed monopolized you all evening."

"No, no, not at all. Helen, I was just thinking—"

"Well, he won't get the chance tonight. We need to catch up on girl talk, don't we? I've missed you so much."

Helen's evident pleasure tipped the scales. Paula hadn't seen Helen since Sam's funeral a year ago. She couldn't disappoint her. "I've missed you, too. I just called to say I'll try to get there early in case there's anything I need to know. I've never chaperoned one of these functions before."

Helen giggled. "Oh, no, dear, there's nothing to it. We just cast stern looks at the students from time to time and try to spot the drunks before they get too obstreperous."

"Okay, thanks," Paula replied. "See you tonight."

After hanging up, she took a long cleansing breath. So she couldn't hide from Boyd. What was one evening?

She spent little time preparing for the dinner dance. She pulled out her favorite gown, one she had bought at Sam's urging, black silk velvet with long sleeves and a sweetheart neckline. The pencil-thin skirt had a long slit up the back, modest yet sophisticated. With her mother's crystal necklace and earrings in place, she felt like Paula Wincott, steeped in the security of her identity. She even felt brave enough to brighten her lips with a wine-red gloss and darken her lashes with smoky mascara. Just before she walked out the door, she sprayed her hair with Sam's favorite perfume. Surrounded by familiarity, she felt confident. And one last glance in the hallway mirror told her she looked dazzling.

She arrived just as the cocktail portion of the evening was winding down and dinner was about to be served. She had never liked cocktails and the ancillary idle conversation, but she loved dancing, and she was sure Helen would share Ed for a dance or two.

From across the room, Helen's friendly voice cut through the din. "Yoo-hoo, Paula, over here."

Paula signaled she was leaving her wrap with the attendant and turned to hand her cloak to the girl at the check stand. Her attention caught on a fur jacket hanging close to the front. It was gorgeous blonde mink cut in a luxurious style with multifaceted stones forming the clasps. She admired its beauty but deplored the cruelty that produced it. She had hoped the animal rights activists had made more of an impact on current thought, but feared there were some callous people who would never get the message.

Ed and Helen appeared at her side. "Paula, my dear, you look ravishing," Helen cooed. "I know you're as old as I, but you've really kept your figure. I'm so jealous."

Paula smiled. She and Helen were indeed the same age, but Helen's pale hair had thinned as her body had thickened, and the only reminder of the young woman inside was the sparkle in her hazel eyes. Ed knew and adored the interior woman, and they enjoyed a romantic relationship despite his seemingly flat personality. Opposites obviously attracted. Paula felt warmed by their company.

"Helen, you're as lovely as you were when I first met you, and you know how much I enjoy you and Ed. Thanks for sharing him this evening."

"Oh, pish," Helen patted her arm, "He just loves all the attention. He's such a party animal."

Ed rolled his eyes at that, then offered an arm to each of them and escorted them in to dinner. As they were being seated, Paula was relieved to see that Boyd Mackenzie was not at their table. She scanned the room, but he was nowhere to be seen. She realized she had been holding her breath, but now she could relax. He had obviously recognized the awkwardness of the situation and decided to avoid any potential for discomfort. She was grateful for the consideration. Perhaps his apology was genuine after all.

She was introduced to the other faculty members seated at their table. Two from organic chemistry were immersed in a conversation about mass spectrometry and carbon fourteen dating. She missed their names. The third was a fresh-faced young woman from biochemistry, along with her fiancé, an associate professor of economics. Introduced as Sandy and Jim, they appeared happy to meet Sam's wife, and she felt immediately comfortable with them. Conversation was easy and interesting, and Paula felt the stress of the past few days release its grasp on her nerves.

Now that she need not fear Boyd's presence, she glanced around to take in her surroundings. The only apparent lighting in the large dining room was from a cluster of amber candles at each of fifty tables, and autumn decorations of gold, red, and brown pulled the room together and made it appear almost cozy. Succulent aromas wafted in from the kitchen as waiters moved silently past the tables carrying heavy trays of roasted game hens, wild rice, cranberry soufflé, and buttery mashed potatoes. A young waiter tipped a toweled-wrapped bottle of champagne into Paula's glass and disappeared as gracefully as he had appeared.

Looking around the table, Ed lifted his glass to make a toast. "To absent friends."

He looked at Paula and smiled. The toast to Sam brought a catch to her throat, as glasses were clicked amidst a chorus of *to absent friends*. She nodded her gratitude to Ed and took a long sip of champagne. It tickled her nose and warmed her throat. The evening was looking up.

Realizing she was hungry, she dug into the appetizing plate set before her. The food was mouth watering. She had never seen some of the exotic side dishes that were passed around the table, but she sampled everything and found them all delicious. With a large contingency of foreign students at the university, the caterer had been encouraged to make use of dishes from representative countries along with the traditional American Thanksgiving specialties.

The noise level of the room was uneven, and, as she looked around, she observed that the tables filled with students emitted bursts of boisterous conversation just short of rowdy.

Ed caught her frown and nodded. "That's what we were like at their age, so I guess we just have to accommodate them—as long as they don't tear the place down."

He had seen more of these affairs than she had, so she deferred to his judgment. Sam wouldn't have been as mellow. He had expected young adults to behave like adults. But Ed was the chairman of the department, and he appeared agreeable to a certain level of indecorous behavior. Helen appeared entirely at ease with the ambiance, and, after a little while, Paula was able to tune it out.

Later, as coffee was being served, the orchestra began to play, and a few couples moved to the dance floor. The music wasn't what she had expected, but she hadn't been to any of these dances while Sam was alive, so she was startled by the volume and rhythm. Couples gyrated and writhed to what sounded like white noise, and her ears were assaulted by the amplifiers.

She was thankful that they were seated away from a loudspeaker when the singer took to the microphone. He wailed something, and the dancers wailed back to him, back and forth, until a clash of cymbals and a long flourish on the electric guitar signaled the end of the number.

She couldn't bring herself to refer to it as a song, but it was obviously appreciated by the young people. At their age, she had been a fan of singers and songwriters who had an ear for melody and wrote real words. Simon and Garfunkel, John Lennon. That was music.

She turned to Helen who sat placidly beside her, spooning chocolate sauce over her Bundt cake and touched her arm. "Is it always like this?

Helen leaned close and turned wide eyes to her. "What?"

"I said, is it always so loud?"

Helen reached both hands under her silver pageboy hairdo and pulled out two spongy earplugs. "Is it too loud for you?"

Paula smothered a laugh. "No, I guess it's just fine." Needing a soother, she emptied the creamer into her coffee and added three lumps of sugar.

After a series of ear blasters, the orchestra finally began a soft rumba, obviously a concession to the old fogies who inhabited the perimeter of the room. Helen stood up, smoothed her blue organza gown, and turned to her husband. She tilted her head in the direction of the dance floor. He arose immediately, twirling her as he led her forward. They were excellent dancers, their movements conditioned by many years of intimacy, and they moved as a single unit across the floor. Sam had never enjoyed dancing, and Paula felt a tiny twinge of disappointment that they had not shared what had always been a love of hers. Ed turned Helen in a particularly intricate move, and she threw her head back gracefully. Ed caught her in his arms, dipped her deeply, and kissed her cheek.

Back at the table, Paula finished her cream-laden, over-sweetened coffee and turned to her dinner companions. One of the young men asked her to dance, and she quickly accepted. Her rumba was rusty, but she was delighted to be on the floor.

When the music ended, Helen caught her hand and held it out to Ed. "Ed, honey, you should dance with Paula."

"With the greatest of pleasure, my dear," he agreed.

Ed took Paula's hand from Helen and led her onto the floor. The band had segued into a familiar Bee Gees tune, and she relaxed. She was less adroit than he, but he held her gently and led her firmly through the basic steps. She felt comfortable with him, and she saw him with new eyes. This was a man of varied accomplishments.

As the strains of music died away, he twirled her, then led her back to their table where she was appalled to find Boyd Mackenzie in an immaculate white dinner jacket standing next to the young biochemistry instructor. She had just introduced him to her fiancé, and they were shaking hands.

His presence wasn't the only shock. Standing at his side was a tall, sleek blonde in a silver lamé gown that left little to the imagination. Her only concession to modesty was a pair of skin-tight evening gloves. She looked to be mid-forties and in the prime of her physical attractiveness. Suddenly Paula felt every one of her years, and each of them paled beside this stunning woman.

Boyd saw her, and his smile was replaced by a look of anxiety. "Paula. Mrs. Wincott. I didn't realize—I was just saying a quick hello to a colleague. We'll be on our way. Sorry to have intruded."

Ed seated Paula, then took Boyd's hand. "Nonsense, my boy. Why don't you join us? Or at least introduce your friend. I do believe that is the lovely Jocelyn, is it not?"

The blonde smiled with Julia Roberts teeth, a white picket fence that stretched from one jeweled ear to the other. Her voice matched her looks, smooth and honeyed. "Hello, Ed. How have you been? How nice to see you, Helen."

Boyd looked uncomfortable, but good manners prevented him from fleeing. "Oh, sorry, yes, Jocelyn Sanders, you know Ed and Helen. You've met everyone except Paula. Mrs. Wincott, another faculty wife, er, widow to be exact."

It was the woman from last Wednesday night. The blonde with the fur jacket. Paula's hand shook as she took the gloved hand ever so briefly. She muttered a perfunctory pleasantry, anxious not to appear ungracious. Jocelyn took Paula's hand and held it warmly. She was difficult to dislike. When she spoke, it was to surprise Paula.

"Of course. You're Sam Wincott's widow. I know all about you. Boyd so admired your husband, Mrs. Wincott, and he respects your hard work and devotion to his work with conductive polymers. I'm not sure I could be so productive in your place." Her mellow voice held a note of complete sincerity that caught Paula off guard.

At that moment, engaged couple Sandy and Jim made their excuses and took an early departure. Ed waved Boyd and Jocelyn to the empty chairs. "Come on, you two, it's been a long time since I've seen Jocelyn. Give us a few minutes to catch up."

With an air of resignation, Boyd seated Jocelyn in the chair next to Ed and took a seat on her other side. After a few moments of chitchat, the music began again. At an adjacent table, a tipsy male voice struggled with *fee - lings...oh, oh, oh...* the beginning strains of *Feelings,* a perennial favorite of the older set. It seemed as if the entire contingent of chaperones moved onto the dance floor at the same time. Ed asked Jocelyn to dance. She moved gracefully as Ed ushered her to the dance floor.

An uneasy silence fell at the table before Helen turned a guileless smile on Boyd. "Since it looks as if your partner has disappeared, I guess you'll have to dance with Paula, won't you?"

They looked at each other blankly. Paula was the first to recover. "Oh, no, Helen, I'd like to sit this one out. You and I haven't chatted in a long time."

Boyd agreed, a little too quickly. "Yes, Helen. We don't see each other often enough. How have you been?"

But Helen remained insistent. "Go on then. Paula loves to dance, Ed's already occupied, and those two," she said, indicating the other two faculty members, "are deep in shop talk. That leaves only you, Boyd. Take her for a spin while I rest my feet."

There was a light in Boyd's eyes that disturbed Paula, and the music was far too romantic, but, when he rose and offered her his hand, she found no legitimate reason to refuse. He led her to the dance floor, slid an arm around her back, and began long, slow steps that moved them smoothly around the floor. He was a superlative dancer, and her movements merged with his effortlessly as he held her a polite distance from his body and turned in fluid circles. Electricity arced between them, flowing easily with the tempo of the music. Slowly, without realizing it, she melted into him.

****

He was in a maelstrom of conflicting emotions. He had been as surprised as she when he found himself kissing her. It hadn't been planned, but desire overcame reason. His telephone apology had been genuine, undertaken after three days of arguing with himself, examining himself and his behavior.

Now, with her in his arms, moving against him as if her body had been designed to fit his arms, he didn't regret it. He had been ambushed by the sight of her tonight, her fulsome body encased in formfitting black, her copper curls only moderately tamed. And the scent of her skin was an aphrodisiac. He wanted to make love to her. That was it, pure and simple. The fact that she was Sam's widow was irrelevant. She was what she was, and he wanted her—to caress her body until she returned his desire, to hold the fullness of her breasts in his hands. With her nails raking his back and her hips rising to meet his, he wanted to fill her with himself and watch her face as she came to orgasm.

Without thinking, he laid his cheek against the top of her head and gathered her more closely against his tautly-aroused body. When she stiffened, he recovered and immediately loosened his grasp. He looked down into her upturned face. Was that passion he saw in her eyes? Could she read the raw hunger he knew was there in his face? She missed a step, and he caught her to regain the rhythm of the dance, but he held her at a barely respectful distance as they continued around the floor.

He knew she was confused. She should be angry that he would hold her so close, but she wasn't. He knew she had felt the hard contours of his erection that pressed against her belly. She had allowed him to kiss her in her home. Had it been a momentary weakness, a temporary need for male companionship?

They stopped dancing and simply held each other in the middle of the dance floor. He stood as frozen as she. His mind numb, he could do nothing but stare at her in confusion.

She hung her head and refused to look at him. "Please." It came out as a whisper.

"Please what?" he answered, his voice strangled.

"What do you want? Why are you doing this to me?"

He dropped his arms at his sides and answered from an anguished heart. "I can't help myself. I want you. With every molecule of my being, I want you in my bed."

They searched each other's faces for what could not be explained by either of them. He knew they were in danger, but she was like a drug to his senses. He fought the impulse to strip her naked and slake himself with her flesh.

Jocelyn's voice brought them back. Ed was escorting her off the dance floor as the orchestra segued into *The Lady in Red*, and she touched Boyd's sleeve with red-lacquered fingernails.

"Boyd, darling, don't forget I have an early plane

tomorrow. We should shake a leg, don't you think?"

Without taking his eyes from Paula's face, he said, "Okay, sure. We can go. I'll get your jacket."

****

Back at the table, Boyd and Jocelyn said their good-byes, and Jocelyn took Boyd's arm. She turned her ravishing smile to Paula. "It was a pleasure to meet you, Paula. I hope to see you again."

Well, it wasn't such a pleasure to meet you.

Jocelyn made her feel old and fat, and her relationship with Boyd was obviously close and of long standing. As he draped the expensive fur jacket around Jocelyn's bare shoulders, she smiled up at him.

Paula felt sick.

CHAPTER TWELVE

Paula went underground again. She avoided visits to the chemistry department office, despite Lottie's invitations to tea. When she did visit Sam's lab, she slipped in and out as quickly as she could. She asked Barry to fax the student work hours to her at home.

"Is anything wrong?" His tone on the telephone was concerned. "Are you sick or something? Do you need anything?"

"No, no, I'm fine. I'm just really busy with my school work. You know how it is. And I'm not as young and bright as I used to be."

She tried to laugh, but it came out a little choked. She hoped he hadn't noticed. "I'm just trying to make maximum use of my time and my fax machine. If you need to talk to me, I'm only a phone call away."

"Sure, I understand. We'll be fine," he comforted. "I'll make sure we fax you the student work hours at the end of each week. Oh, hey, by the way, Dr. King says he saw the grant applications and they're killer. He thinks we have a good chance of getting funding from more than one source. Wouldn't that be great?"

"Yes, that's great."

But even such good news couldn't lift her malaise. She was mired in something bigger than herself, and had to think it through. She felt like a character in an overblown Italian movie where individuals indulged passions without regard to reason. High drama was not a part of her life, and illicit romantic entanglements were unthinkable.

Her life was delineated by her name, her family, and her responsibility, but a moment alone with Boyd was enough to distort her vision of herself and create a woman she didn't know and didn't like. She had to restore herself to an even keel, and to do that she had to avoid any contact with him. He was as much her nemesis as he had been Sam's.

One afternoon just before Christmas break she heard the answering machine pick up. Lottie's voice sang out.

"Paula, I'm calling to see if you're okay, hon. My little brown betty and I are still here, and I'd love to have a girl chat. I have some good news, and I'm just bursting to share it with someone. Give me a call when you have some free time, and we can get together. I'm at the office."

Paula picked up the telephone. "I haven't been around to see you. I've just been so darned busy. You know, the life of a student who hasn't been in school for a very long time."

She tried to sound light. "What's this news you're bursting to tell?"

"I'm getting married. Come to tea at four o'clock today, and I'll tell you all about it. I'm so excited. Can you make it?"

Paula was floored. Lottie getting married? Lottie? For this kind of news she was willing to take her chances of running into Boyd. "I'm on my way."

She pulled on tan cowboy boots over her jeans, threw on her heavy red coat, and grabbed the car keys. This was worth a trip to the campus.

The teakettle was already whistling when she stepped into the office. Lottie wasn't at her desk, and the aroma of cinnamon wafted from the lounge. "Lottie, it's Paula. Are you in the back?"

Her friend's ebullient mood was evident in her voice. "Yes, dear, come on back. I'm just making the tea."

Paula took off her coat and tossed it onto the closest chair. She crossed into the faculty lounge, sank into the cushioned sofa, and waited impatiently for Lottie to finish her preparations. At last the dark Irish tea was steeping, and the ubiquitous coffeecake lay in mountainous portions. Lottie had even added a bowl of deep yellow butter and a jar of thick clover honey.

Paula reached for a cup and held it up to Lottie. As she did so, she noticed that Lottie's face was aglow. She was positively radiant. Even her movements were more graceful. Gone was the lumbering gait and the image of an overweight, middle-aged matron.

Paula's mouth dropped, and, when she had recovered herself, she couldn't refrain from articulating surprise. "Who is this gorgeous woman I see before me? And what is that beautiful outfit you're wearing? You've been doing some serious shopping."

Lottie dipped her head and smiled shyly. The shapeless shift she had always worn had been replaced by a mauve angora sweater set with pearl buttons. Her matching wool skirt fit perfectly and gave a professional line to her generous figure. Her grey hair had been cut in a short bob, and it sparkled silver in the low afternoon sun. Lottie was transformed. She ran her hands swiftly over her skirt, and then sat down opposite Paula. She poured two cups of tea, then inched forward in her chair. "Do I look okay? I so want to look nice for him, but I'm out of practice. And I feel a little silly trying to spruce myself up at my age."

Too interested in Lottie's news to eat cake, Paula downed a big gulp of tea before she bombarded Lottie with questions. "Come on, give. Who is he? Where did you meet him? How long have you known him? And, my dear, whatever could you be thinking?"

Surely Lottie was too old for such frivolity. She was good old reliable Lottie, a fixture in the department ever since Paula could remember. How could she get married? It had never occurred to Paula that Lottie might have a life outside the university. Now she was getting married.

"His name is James McTaggart. He owns the company that services the Xerox machines, and he's a fine figure of a man, if I do say so myself. I've known him for—I don't know, maybe ten years. But he was married, so I never paid him much mind. I only ever saw him when he came round to try to convince us to upgrade our machines."

She relaxed a little and leaned on the arm of the chair. "But a couple of years ago he lost his wife. He was mighty torn up for a long time. He loved her a lot, you know, and they'd been married over thirty years. I think it was some lingering illness that took her, so he lost her little by little. Very sad."

"And—" Paula prompted, impatient to get to the marriage proposal.

"And about six months ago he came in on one of his visits, and we got to talking. I don't think I ever told you, but I lost my fiancé in an auto accident when I was a young woman, so we had something in common. We just talked. Then he started coming in a bit more often, and finally he asked me to have a cup of coffee. We went over to the cafeteria and just sat for a time, getting to know one another. And, after a few coffee chats, he asked me out to dinner."

She placed a palm on each cheek to hide her blush.

"Oh, Paula, I was so nervous. I hadn't had a date in so many years I thought I'd forgotten how to do it." She giggled, and Paula felt a twinge of irritation.

Lottie's words didn't make sense. This man had

been devoted to his wife for thirty years, and now he was going to forget all about her and marry Lottie? Not that Lottie wasn't a wonderful person, entirely deserving of every happiness, but hadn't she passed her prime? Wasn't this a mistake that both would regret? Weren't they simply too old for this kind of recklessness?

"I'm sure he's a wonderful man, but have you thought this through? You could be making a big mistake. How old is he?"

Lottie peered over the top of her glasses. "What possible difference could his age make?" She gave a slight shrug. "He's about my age, I guess. We never talked about it."

Confounded, Paula asked, "How could you not have talked about it? You're not a young girl anymore."

Cup in mid air, Lottie tilted her head to one side. "I'm not sure I follow you."

"I'm saying that you may be overreacting. You know, wild romanticism is part and parcel of youth." When she saw an odd look in Lottie's eyes, she tried to backpedal. "I mean, the blood cools a bit when people reach our age, don't you think?"

Lottie's deep, hearty laugh punctuated her answer. "Why, I never heard that. As a matter of fact my blood comes near to boiling every time I look at him. And the things he says to me make my face turn red."

Paula couldn't believe what she was hearing. She wanted to stuff her fingers in her ears, but Lottie was oblivious. "He's everything I ever wanted in a man. He says he loves me, and I believe him. I get goose bumps when I hear his voice, and when he touches me I feel lightheaded. He's asked me to marry him, and we're setting the date."

"But, don't you see? He's already had a wife, someone he loved with all of his heart. You can't hope to replace her."

Lottie looked as if Paula had lost her mind. "And why would I be trying to replace her? That he loved her is a beautiful thing. How sad his life would have been if he hadn't had love. I'm not sure I understand what you're trying to say."

Paula set her face in a stern look and warned, "I'm just trying to get you to see the reality of the situation. You know I'm very fond of you, and I don't want to see you get hurt. This sounds like a flight of fancy with a man who's having a mid-life crisis or something."

"Oh, now, don't you worry about that." Lottie forked a piece of coffee cake into her mouth, chewed a bit, and continued, "My Jamie had his mid-life crisis years ago, and now he's very clear on how he wants to spend the rest of his life. He's going to sell his business, and we're going to live in his house in Aspen. He likes to ski, and he says he'll teach me." She giggled again. "Can't you just see me on the bunny slope? I've never been on skis in my life, but I'm game to try."

Lottie put down her cup and took Paula's hands. "I want you to be my matron of honor. Will you? It would mean a lot to me, and, once you meet my Jamie, I know you'll love him. I'll work until the end of April, then we're planning the wedding for May. After that, it's married life for me."

"You're quitting your job? But everyone relies on you."

"Oh, I'm sure they'll rely on someone else soon enough."

She looked so happy, Paula couldn't be unkind. She capitulated gracefully. "Of course I'll be your matron on honor, Lottie. I'm very glad for you, and I look forward to meeting your man. I'm sure he's everything you say he is."

Paula left the chemistry office with a heavy

heart. She was sincerely happy for Lottie but sad for herself. She was losing another beam in the framework that had been her life in Boulder. She felt as if a giant hand had grasped her life, turned it upside down, and was shaking it, pieces falling out one by one. Tears stuck in the back of her throat as she drove back to her empty house.

But Christmas was coming, and she could lose herself in Ben and Chloe's excitement. It was like having Emma and Morgan little again, except now she could indulge the grandchildren as she had never indulged her own children. Sam had always warned her not to give them too much lest they come to expect too much from life and suffer disappointment. She didn't really understand his philosophy, but she acceded to it because Sam knew much more about everything than she did. Now that he was no longer here to admonish her, she could give free reign to her impulses and make Christmas a magical time for the children.

As she turned off Baseline Drive, soft snowflakes began to fall—big, fat, fluffy ones that sat on her coat, displaying their uncanny designs for a split second before melting. She waited every year for the first snowfall, and this one was as beautiful as she had ever seen. When she parked her car, she stood outside for a few minutes, watching the play of snowflake patterns on the suede of her coat in that instant before they melted and disappeared as if they had never been. Something stirred in her, something unidentifiable, something profoundly sad.

****

High in the exquisite mountains of Estes Park, Boyd watched the snow drop onto the skylights of his getaway cabin. Since the disaster at the Thanksgiving dance, he, too, had gone underground, or rather to the high ground. His feelings for Paula had gained a momentum he was unable to understand or control. He found her undeniably desirable, and her dedication to her husband was admirable. She was bright, articulate, and that head of red curls held a temper. God, she was beautiful when she was fired up. She had loved Sam with all the ardor of the young, but how could he convince her that her life was not over and that ardor belongs to all ages? And, moreover, should he interfere in the life that she created and in which she found contentment?

He picked up a poker and pushed another log into the fireplace. Without conscious intent, his imagination conjured a vision of her in front of the fire, flushed with a warm brandy, a fine dew on her naked flesh, and her lips moist and inviting. He shook his head and finished off his cup of tepid black coffee.

A car honked in front of the cabin, and Boyd opened the front door to see Jocelyn exiting the driver's side and waving him to come out. "Put on your boots and help me with the luggage. I've a trunk filled with presents, so get a move on. It's cold out here."

He grabbed his sheepskin jacket from the peg and pulled on his boots. The snow crunched under his feet, and the air was crisp and dry. It was a flawless Colorado winter day. Jocelyn loaded him with valises, and she carried brightly-wrapped gifts into the cabin.

She stopped just inside the door and whistled. "Hey, what's all this? You've done some major work on this place; I'd recognize your style anywhere. And it looks beautiful."

She glanced around the spacious cabin. It was more like an expensive but rustic house, inhabitable year round. It comprised two full bedrooms and a sleeping loft, a large kitchen with an island, industrial gas stove and two ovens, and large den with a massive stone fireplace and a stadium-sized plasma television set. Bachelor heaven.

She dropped the presents in the nearest plush leather chair and turned to look at him. His sober demeanor did not diminish his rugged good looks, but she sensed an unusual restlessness in him. His blue eyes had lost the sparkle she had come to know and the sensuous lips no longer curved up at the edges quite so readily.

But dressed in jeans and a red and white alpine sweater, he was still the best looking middle-aged hunk she knew. She threw her arms around his neck and hugged him close. "Merry Christmas, darling. What are you drinking?"

He patted her back and waited to be released. "I've just had coffee, but I can fix you a hot toddy, or I think I have some eggnog in the fridge. What's your choice?"

He moved to the kitchen, set his coffee cup on the counter, and opened the cupboard. She kicked off expensive red leather boots and began picking up the presents from the chair. "A hot toddy, please. I'll just put the presents under the tree, shall I?"

An eight-foot fully-decorated Scotch pine held court in the corner. Quaint, carved, hand-painted balls and intricate Christmas-themed decorations hung from every limb, and ropes of gold tinsel looped around the tree from bottom to top. At the pinnacle, a frail, gauzy angel displayed her open wings. The scent of freshly-cut pine permeated the cabin and mixed with the aroma of logs cracking in the fireplace.

She had heard him speak lovingly of his getaway, but she had no idea it would be so striking, so thoroughly masculine. It fit him perfectly, and she understood his love for the place.

She nodded slowly, "I'm impressed."

After carefully placing the gifts under the tree

amongst the many that already graced the corner, she took her hot toddy and sank down on the rug in front of the fireplace. "No wonder you like to escape up here. It's absolutely grand. You must find it hard to go back to Boulder and the university after spending a couple of weeks up here, especially when the snow falls. It's like a fairytale."

He settled himself in a leather seat and warmed his hands before the fire. "You're welcome to come up as often as you want. I'll give you a set of keys. It's just a matter of making the time. If you weren't so busy with your practice, you could spend a lot more time of here."

"Oh, I know. It's just that we're a small firm, and, with my heavy caseload, I can't just take off whenever the fancy strikes me. But, I promise you, I'll certainly make more of an effort, now that I've seen the place."

She sat for a moment, sipping her hot toddy. He stared into the fire. A log hissed and crackled in the silence. No one moved.

"Penny for your thoughts."

He turned to her with a grimace. "You'd be getting the short end of the stick, I'm afraid. My thoughts haven't been worth much lately. I can't seem to think clearly since—"

"Since?"

He shook his head.

She laid a hand on his arm to get his attention. "That woman, Paula Wincott, the one I met at the dance. Who is she?"

He clasped both hands and placed them between his knees. He leaned forward, resting his elbows on his thighs, and hesitated slightly before responding. "She's Sam Wincott's widow. I only just met her in September."

"Uh huh." She waited for him to continue.

"Sam never brought her around to any of the

department functions, so she's been quite a surprise—to all of us."

"Boyd, you know what I'm asking. Don't dodge the question."

He shrugged, "She's a student. She was signed up for my two-oh-one section. That's where I met her. But she dropped it the same day. Something about scheduling." Cornered by Jocelyn's prodding look, he continued, "Well, actually, to be completely honest, she and I have seen each other a few times so we could dig up money to keep Sam's lab going. Didn't I tell you all this before?"

She smiled indulgently. "I know what you told me, but I also know what I observed when you looked at her."

"How did I look at her?"

"And I heard your voice crack when you introduced us. You might as well have a neon sign hung around your neck."

"That obvious?"

"Yes, it's that obvious."

He rested his head in his hands and released a profound sigh. "This is such a mess. I didn't expect— I mean, she's not what I would have expected to..." He rubbed his forehead. "I can't explain what I don't understand. I only know there's a combustion when I'm near her, and I'm afraid I'll make a fool of myself."

Jocelyn's eyes widened. "Oh, my goodness, it's much worse than I thought." She set her mug down. Then, sitting back on her heels, turned to face him. "I figured it was just some mild flirtation with the widow woman down the street, but this sounds ominous. Do you think this is a good idea?"

"Obviously not."

"What are you going to do?"

"She says because Sam hated me, she must hate me. She's getting in the way of her own life, holding onto bitterness that doesn't belong to her. I don't know if she would ever have responded to me, even if Sam hadn't been in the picture. But I'll never know, because he's still in the picture and will always be. I can't compete with a dead hero."

He smiled at Jocelyn. "Sorry, kid, I didn't mean to get off on this subject. You caught me off guard." He took her hands and stood up, pulling her to her feet. "Hey, I have big, thick steaks and a mountain of potatoes. How about if we make one helluva dinner?"

Jocelyn laughed, then headed for the kitchen. "Sounds like a great idea. I brought a Black Forest cake and vanilla ice cream. Let's be baaaaaaad."

Loud banging on the door signaled the arrival of Reid Mackenzie, his presence announced by a blast of cold wind and a great shaking of snow off his down-filled parka. The snorkel hood obscured his face, but the voice that bellowed from beneath his muffler could be no other.

"Hey you in there, I'm starving. And I need a hot drink." He set his suitcase down and pushed back the hood from his face, a face that strongly resembled Boyd but was not as lean. His eyes were a lighter shade of blue, the face was full and boyish, and his body was a little fuller, but they were clearly brothers.

Boyd clasped him in a bear hug, and they vigorously patted each other's shoulders and backs, raising great clouds of snow from Reid's parka. "Hey, little brother, thank God you're here. I need you to rescue me. This wife of yours has been giving me the third degree and making me spill my guts to her. I have no privacy at all."

Reid took off his parka and handed it to Boyd with a wry grin. "She does have a way of getting in under your radar. I guess I shouldn't have married a lawyer, but she sure does make good money. Fact is, I'm thinking of retiring early and just sitting back drinking Margaritas while she earns the bread."

He shook his head and brushed the hair back from his forehead, hair that was a shade darker than Boyd's but graying at the temples. "I could just kick back and enjoy life."

Jocelyn appeared at his elbow with a hot toddy. "Are you two talking about me? Generous praise, I hope."

She gave Reid a lingering kiss on the mouth before handing him a drink. "Darling, you're early. I thought your plane didn't get in for another hour."

Reid took a long swig of his drink. "I decided to cancel the graduate seminar and let my students go home early. They didn't have their minds on European history and I wanted to get a jump on the weather. How did the filing go?"

"Slam dunk. I thought I'd have to spend at least one night in D.C., but I caught a window and got it all done in a day."

Jocelyn pushed up the sleeves of her pink turtleneck sweater. "We're just about to put on steaks, my darling, so your timing is excellent."

Reid slipped an arm around her waist and nuzzled her neck. "Isn't it always?"

Boyd tossed a salad while the steaks broiled and Jocelyn monitored the potatoes baking in the microwave. Dinner was warm and cozy, and Boyd was in the company of the two people he loved most in the world—his only brother and the woman who had made that brother sublimely happy. When Reid had first introduced them, Boyd had thought Jocelyn too glamorous and high powered to be the wife of a modest college professor in Florida, but, after twenty years of wedded bliss, they had proved him wrong. They clearly adored each other and had a sexually-charged, romantic relationship that Boyd envied.

He watched them together and was happy for them. But he also longed for that kind of relationship himself. He wanted it with Paula. The realization thudded through his body with a power he couldn't control. But desire clashed with reality and he knew he couldn't make her love him just because he wanted it.

CHAPTER THIRTEEN

Christmas with the family acted as a tonic for Paula's spirits. The lengthy term paper for World Literature required many hours of research and organization, but the reward was an A on the paper, and a B+ on the final exam. With a renewed energy to pour into her studies, she signed up for Professor Sloan's section of Biochemistry 201, and added a course in Dramatic Literature that looked promising. For insurance, and to make Emma proud, she might avail herself of chemistry tutorials.

She liked to think Sam would be proud of her, too. Whenever she thought of him, more and more she felt him slipping away—as Boyd intruded. She remembered Sam's inner spirit in those early years, but his face was obscured. She struggled to recapture his image, to force Boyd from her mind. Boyd, the rival who had totally demoralized Sam in the last five years of his life, so totally that nothing mattered except bitterness. She had been robbed of five years of joy with her husband. And Boyd was responsible.

Why than was he so willing to help Sam's project? Why did he disclaim any awareness of rivalry? Why had he been so kind to Ben?

Why was his touch so arousing?

Had she become the archetypal widow looking for a quick roll in the hay? Life had become so terribly complicated, and nothing in her previous years had prepared her.

She threw herself into her studies hoping to block Boyd from her mind at least long enough to finish the Spring semester. Then he would be rotated back to back to graduate-level courses. The paperwork for the grant application was complete, and there was no legitimate reason for them to meet. If she avoided all faculty functions, she could keep him at bay. Then temptation and the accompanying guilt would be out of her life, and she could resume her identity as Sam Wincott's wife.

****

Such was not to be. One Friday night, as she prepared study sheets for biochemistry, the front doorbell rang. When Paula opened the door, there he stood in a navy pea jacket with the collar turned up. He looked tired. A five o'clock shadow darkened his cheeks, and his hair was rumpled. Without preamble, he declared, "We have to talk."

Paula's heart jumped into her throat, but knew he was right. The time had come to put cards on the table. She couldn't keep ducking and hiding for the rest of her life.

She ushered him into the den where the fireplace threw soft light onto the plush furnishings. A pot of hot chocolate rested on the coffee table. The computer rolled in screen-saver mode. She took his jacket and laid it across the desk where she had been working, then motioned for him to take a large armchair. Seating herself opposite him in a matching armchair, she tried to quell the jumble in her brain. They sat silently for a long minute, each assessing the other, looking for an opening.

"Paula," he began, but she cut him off.

She had to blurt out before she lost her nerve. He was too appealing in the firelight. His physical presence assaulted her senses and made it difficult to think clearly.

"I know I may have been a little unreasonable, but you have to understand my position. It's possible you may not be the great demon Sam believed you to be, but I'm his wife, my loyalty is to him. If he was unhappy because of you, then you must see that I can't pretend nothing was wrong between you."

He moved his chair a hair closer to hers. His hands shook, she noticed. He clasped them together on his knees. "This is awkward for both of us." He glanced at the table. "Do you think I could have a cup of whatever is in that pot, just so I have something to do with my hands?"

She didn't want to offer him anything, but he appeared as nervous as she. She poured out two mugs of steaming hot cocoa, handed one to him, taking care not to touch his fingers, and seated herself back in the chair before the fire. She put her mug on the footstool in front of her chair, but couldn't drink it. Her stomach felt too knotted up to accept it.

He blew on the cocoa before taking a sip. When he spoke at last, his voice was low but clear. "Yes, you've been unreasonable. No, I don't understand your position. I'm not the great demon. And you're not Sam's wife. So let's see if we can iron out some of the unnecessary problems we're having."

He held the cup in his lap and look into her face. "As I told you before, I had no idea Sam was unhappy nor that I was the cause of it. Whatever ill will he harbored toward me was of his own making, and I never felt anything toward him but admiration."

He rose to stand before the fire for a moment. He gazed into the fire to gather his thoughts. Then he set his mug on the mantle and turned to face her. "You can't in good conscience blame me for his bitterness. He was the architect of his own feelings. Whatever was wrong, it was on his side."

She sat up, shoulders stiffened. "Are you insinuating there was something wrong with my husband?"

He shook his head, clearly impatient with her refusal to understand. "Not at all. He was everything you said. We did not have bad blood between us. If he disliked me, Paula, the feeling was not mutual, so you'll have to have to deal with that. Think about it. What have I done to make you or Sam hate me? Tell me."

The insistence in his tone intimidated her.

"I know he spoke of you as if you were the devil set out to destroy him. Every time he had a problem at work, he found a reason to blame you. I thought you two were in open conflict. What you're telling me is hard to believe."

Boyd leaned imperceptibly forward. "Paula, ask anyone who knew us. Ask Lottie or Ed if we ever had conflict, personal or professional. There was never a negative word between us. I'm truly sorry Sam felt threatened by me. I'm sorry for him, but I'm more sorry for you. It's poisoned your perspective, and I don't believe that's what he intended."

She ran her fingers through her hair, then clasped her hands in her lap. "Whatever his perspective, as his wife I must be loyal to that. I can't just throw away all of those years. Don't you understand?"

"You're not throwing anything away. You had all of those wonderful years with Sam. They were real."

He moved her cocoa to the floor and sat on the footstool before her. He didn't touch her, but he spoke in a tone that carried powerful conviction. "You're not Sam Wincott's wife any longer. You're a widow, and loyalty to a dead man is misplaced if it keeps you from having a life. Do you think that's what he would have wanted for you? You had a long, fruitful, and rich life with Sam. But he's gone, and you're still here. You didn't die with him, and you have to live whatever time you have left—as we all do. I'm not trying to take his place; no one could do that."

She heard the catch in his breath as he lightly touched the back of her hand with a forefinger. When she didn't shake him off, he began stroking in tiny circles. "You went back to school because you're still a vibrant woman with years ahead of you that should be filled with life and joy."

His breathing quickened, but he kept his eyes on her hand, turned it palm upward, and continued the circles. "There's something between us, Paula. You know it, and I know it. I don't know what it is exactly, but I want to give it a chance. From that first day, I wanted to lock the classroom door and make love to you on my desk. I know you feel something for me, Paula. Your hand is trembling as I touch you."

It was true, her hand was trembling, and where his finger touched, the flesh felt scalded. Heavy honey began to flow through her veins, and she became lightheaded. He dipped his head and replaced his finger with his lips. His tongue continued the tiny circles in the middle of her palm. A ragged cry escaped her, and with her other hand she grasped his hair.

He slid his hands around her waist and moved his mouth to her throat. He lifted her sweater slightly and rubbed his face against the bare skin of her belly. The stubble of his beard excited every nerve ending until she was on fire. His tongue moved upwards toward her breasts and then down, down. He raised his head to look into her face, and she gave him what he had been searching for. She wanted him.

He reached for her mouth. She leaned to meet him. The merge was electric. She made no attempt to resist him. She wrapped her arms around his shoulders and leaned toward him as he pulled her from her chair, onto the carpet before the fire. He fell back and pulled her on top of him, and every inch of their bodies melted into each other as the kiss sucked the marrow from her bones.

She was unprepared for the volley of physical sensations he evoked and the intensity of her response. He spread his thighs and trapped her body between them, forcing her firmly against his arousal. He was full and hot, even through the denim of his jeans, and she moved against him slowly, unaware that she was doing so. Her body had a purpose of its own.

He broke the kiss. "That feels too good. I've been erect for hours. Just thinking about seeing you tonight, I might explode, I want you too much."

He rolled her onto her side and raised her sweater. The vision of her bare breasts almost pushed him over the edge then and there. Full and round, and the rosy nipples beckoned to him. He allowed one breast to fall into the palm of his hand, and began circling the nipple with his thumb, just enough to elicit a husky moan from her. He squeezed gently as she watched the play of porcelain flesh under the tan skin of his hand. The contrast excited her, and when he claimed the nipple with his lips, pinpricks raced along every nerve in her body. His mouth sucked while his hand continued to knead the breast, his tongue circled the aureole, and his teeth nipped, all the while he gathered more of her flesh into his mouth—he a starving man, she a sumptuous feast.

Paula held his head against her body and arched her back. Lost in an ecstasy she had forgotten—or had never known—she was unaware when he lifted the sweater over head and flung it away. She knew only that he now held both breasts in his hands while his mouth, his glorious mouth, had moved to the other nipple to repeat the sucking and nipping while his hands continued stroking.

"You're so beautiful. I'm about to lose it just by touching you. I want to make it good for you, but I'm not sure I can take my time."

His mouth returned to hers while his hands worked the zipper on her jeans, breaking the kiss only long enough to pull them from her long legs. Then his kiss was on her belly and moving lower. He paused at a tiny scar, which he seemed to find intensely erotic, kissing it repeatedly before continuing his journey down her body. Downy auburn curls peeked through silky white panties, and when his mouth reached the apex of her thighs, he slowly licked her through the cloth. She squirmed and raised her hips to meet his mouth.

"You taste so delicious, I must have it all. Open for me."

She sighed, and her legs came apart, an invitation that spurred him to greater intimacy. He mouthed her over and over again, until the panties were wet and transparent, then he returned to kiss her breasts while his hand covered her and a finger moved under the edge of her panties to caress the soft hair that now showed clearly through the sheer fabric. She turned cloudy green eyes to him and read desire that mirrored her own. He covered her with his palm and slid a finger inside her. As his finger moved slowly in and out, his thumb rubbed an insistent circle over her clitoris. Her hips began a rhythmic motion of their own.

"Yes." She groaned, then panted, helpless against the urgency of ruthless, carnal need building and threatening to overflow.

He smiled at her response. The moment had come. "That's it, sweetheart. You're wet for me, and I'm hard for you. We're right for each other. Let me in."

Her breathing turned to soft cries. She reached

for him, rubbing her hand against the zipper of his jeans. "I want you naked. I want to see you."

As if waiting for her to ask, he pulled off his sweatshirt and unzipped his jeans, but she reached inside to grasp him before he could remove the jeans. He was hot and hard, and he grunted when she squeezed the erect object of her desire. He kicked off his jeans and peeled off his jockey underwear. He stood before her as if offering himself to her.

She was unable to take her eyes from his body. The firelight turned his skin to bronze, and he was male beauty personified. She already knew his shoulders and torso were muscular and a mat of salt and pepper hair covered his chest. But her mouth went dry when her eyes followed that line of hair down his body into a dark thatch that crowned his penis. Long and thick, proudly erect, and it seemed to pulsate as she reached for it. An answering heat arose within the depths of her own body. She sat up to take him in both hands, but he pushed her back to the carpet.

"No, wait, there's something else first. I don't want this be over too fast. I want it to be good for both of us, slow and good. I could make love to you all night and still not have enough."

He laid her on her back and licked his way down her body. She was shocked when he pulled her legs over his shoulders and, with one hand, ripped the frail panties from her body. He grasped her under the hips, pulled her to his waiting mouth, and buried his tongue in her, groaning, grunting, as if to devour her. Something primitive in his lovemaking struck an answer in her, igniting a fire that raced through her body, culminating in the sensitive spot where his tongue and teeth created havoc. As her nervous system reached overload, she clenched both hands in his thick hair to hold him against her, tugging at him, keening, nearly unconscious from the vividness of sheer sensation.

****

He was beyond knowing or caring about anything except the aroma, the taste, the feel of the woman beneath him. Urgency overcame him. His body had been ready for her body for months, and denial had honed his desire to a fever pitch. Delicious agony danced through his veins as he delayed the inevitable plunge into the sweetness of her, and he couldn't have stopped if his life had been forfeit. With his mouth still sucking her softness, he reached up to take her breasts in both hands, softly squeezing and rolling the nipples between his thumbs and forefingers. He touched her everywhere, and he gloried in her eager response. Her hands in his hair and the moans deep in her throat urged him on.

"Now," she gasped. "Please, now."

From far away he heard her voice and knew the moment had come. He slid up her body, pausing only to take another bite from a turgid nipple. Then, with a choked cry, he entered her, deeply, strongly, fully. He meant to wait a moment to accustom her to his size, but she wrapped silken thighs around him, and he had no choice. His body acted without his will, and as his hips pounded into her, she rose to meet each thrust, keeping him tightly sheathed in her as her hands captured and held his buttocks, assuring him with strangled cries of "Yes, yes, yes."

As her head tossed from side to side, he kissed her neck, licking the perspiration from her skin. His chest rubbed against her breasts, and the friction added yet another layer of sensuality. Their senses vibrated like tightly-strung wire as they raced toward the inevitable yet trying to hold onto the tension as long as possible, blind to everything except each other.

He watched her climb, he saw the moment her

eyes reflected the shock of climax. Her lids fluttered as she arched and bucked, shattering his control. He plunged hard into her, shouting his pleasure as she buried her face in his shoulder. They clutched each other as their bodies shook with the force of the orgasm. He felt pleasure-pain as her teeth met his skin and her mouth sucked his flesh, all the while keening a long cry of release. He pounded into her again and again as she clutched his hips and pulled him to her.

As the force began to subside, they rocked together, slowly falling from the heights as they felt their heartbeats gradually slow. For a long time they lay together, still wrapped in each other's arms. At last he felt his heart return to a semblance of normal, although he knew he would never be normal again, and he stroked her sweat-dampened hair very, very gently.

"Are you still in there?"

She took a long breath, then sighed, "I don't know who's in here, but it's not Paula. Some sex-crazed woman took over temporarily, and I fear she behaved like a nymphomaniac. I'm so embarrassed."

When he laughed, his belly rubbed against hers. A wondrous sensation that—naked flesh on naked flesh. "Whoever she was, could I please make her acquaintance? I like her a lot." He paused to look at her straight on. "And I think she likes me."

"It's been a long time. Maybe I'm just the typical lonely widow that everyone makes fun of. I've never felt anything like that in my life, and I truly don't know who I am or what I'm doing. Having sex with a virtual stranger is not my style."

He nuzzled the side of her mouth. "You're not having sex with a virtual stranger, Paula. You're making love with a man who's been besotted with you for months." He gave a little push to remind her he was still inside her. "And it was amazing. You'd be a liar to say it wasn't."

"I won't deny it was beyond anything I could have imagined, but it must be your skill. I've been married all of my adult life, so I don't have a wide range of experience, but you took me somewhere I've never been." She toyed with the hair on his chest and blushed. "Yes, I admit it really was amazing."

He slowly withdrew from her body and pulled her into a seated position on the carpet. He leaned against a chair, opened his legs, and drew her close to him, laying her head against his chest.

"It wasn't me; it was us. We created that experience together, from who we are and what we are together. We're magnets that can't resist each other, two matches that ignite when struck together, and it was destiny that we should meet and make love. Do you believe that?"

She dipped her head against his question. "I don't know. I don't know what I believe anymore. I thought I knew myself. But I just proved that theory wrong. I feel as if I'm two people. One Paula is Sam's wife, Emma and Morgan's mother, Ben and Chloe's grandmother, domestic and tranquil, conservative and predictable."

She pulled his arms more snugly around her, and her voice dropped. "The other Paula is completely different, a wild woman who wants to sing and paint nudes and make love among the wildflowers. The new Paula frightens the old one." She shook her head slowly. "How can I explain her?"

"You don't have to," he whispered. "Unleash her. Let her run free until she finds her place. Water seeks its own level, but you've been dammed up for all these years, so you have a lot of time to make up. Let me help."

He put his hand under her chin and tipped her head back to look into her eyes. "We're so good together. Let me show you it wasn't a mistake. It'll be better and better every time."

A tiny glint appeared in her eyes, and her hand reached between his legs. "Maybe you could show me right now."

She began to stroke him, and he rewarded her with a quick lengthening and hardening that took her entire attention. "Look what you've done," he said with a smile. "You must be the new Paula. What a pleasure to meet you."

"The pleasure is all mine," she murmured as she laid her head in his lap and applied her mouth to the task, nibbling, lapping, and finally taking him into her mouth.

He grasped the sides of her head and held her while she continued her ministrations until—"I can't stand it. Come here."

He pulled her to him and sat her on his lap facing him, impaling her, filling her with hot desire. She wrapped her arms around his neck, her legs around his waist, and threw her head back as he held her hips and thrust upwards into her. He filled his mouth with one ripe breast, tugging strongly, then reached for her lips. They kissed frantically, each trying to envelop the other.

It was only a long while later, after the fire had burned itself out on the hearth, that they lay at last in each other's arms, sated.

****

Paula was the first to come to her senses. She made a move to rise, but he tightened his arms around her. "Don't go," he muttered. "Stay with me."

"It's cold. The fire's out."

He threw a leg over hers. "My fire's not out, only smoldering. Don't get up; let's enjoy the afterglow."

"All right, but let's get warm." She drew a fuzzy afghan off the sofa and wrapped it around them, then settled back into his arms. He grunted his approval and rolled their bodies together.

With growing children in the house for such a long time, lovemaking with Sam was conditioned by the possibility of intrusion at any moment. With afterglow being a luxury they couldn't afford, it never became a part of their intimacy. Now, with complete privacy and a man who was in no hurry, she found it completely enchanting. He stroked her arm and kissed her cheek, murmuring something unintelligible, then he turned her so they were spooned beneath the afghan, and he held her for a long time. Time was out of joint, but she didn't care. This moment was precious, one to be savored.

CHAPTER FOURTEEN

Paula wakened hours later with Boyd's arm still around her. A glance at her watch told her it was well past midnight. She came up on her knees and began searching for her sweater and jeans.

He opened a sleepy eye and caught her wrist. "What is it? What's the matter?"

She pulled free of his grasp. "Nothing's the matter; it's just really late. You have to go." She found her sweater and pulled it over her head. "It's after midnight."

He rubbed his eyes, then sat up. "Why do I have to go? I want to be with you all night. I want to have breakfast with you tomorrow." He leaned his elbows on his knees and watched her, making no move to leave. "I make a mean Denver omelet if I do say so myself."

She located her jeans, then rose to step into them. The torn panty was nowhere to be found. "You can't spend the night. I can't have the neighbors speculating on what's going on here. I don't even know what's going on."

"You're a grown woman, a single, middle-aged woman, for God's sake. Why would you care that the neighbors think you had a man overnight? That's what grown-up single people do."

"I don't know what single people do. I've never been single. This was an aberration of some sort, and you absolutely have to go."

"But—"

"I mean it, Boyd." She handed him his sweatshirt, then began searching the floor for the rest of his clothes. "Where are your jeans? Were you wearing boots?"

"Okay, okay, don't rush me."

He unwrapped himself from the blanket and slipped into his underwear and jeans. She spied his boots sticking out from under the sofa and pushed them over to where he could reach them. He tugged them on while she returned the afghan to the sofa.

"I thought we had made some progress, come to some kind of understanding. My God, woman, we just made love—twice. Doesn't that mean anything to you?"

But she was already fetching his jacket from the desk and putting it into his hands. "Of course it means something to me. I just don't know what. You have to give me some time to think about what took place here. And you may not spend the night in Sam's bed."

He shrugged into his jacket, ran a hand through his hair, then turned to take her in his arms. "I'd sooner use it for kindling before I'd sleep in it. But to be with you, I'd sleep right here on the floor. Just to hold you in my arms all night, I'd be happy to sleep on the sofa. I'm going to be in your life, that's a given, so you're going to have to make space for me."

She tried to speak, but he shushed her. "I'm not some one-night stand you can hump and dump. Now, kiss me properly, and I'll go—for now, but I'll be back. You can count on it."

He clasped her head with one hand and gathered her into a close embrace. His kiss weakened her knees, but she held onto her resolve, even when his hand cupped her breast and squeezed.

She rushed him through the door, but just before she closed it behind him, he turned to her with a secret smile and tossed back, just loud enough for the neighbors to hear, "I hope you'll be sore tomorrow."

She shut the door firmly. Boyd was incorrigible, and she was embarrassed. On her way down the hall, she caught a glimpse of herself in the wall mirror and saw to her chagrin that she had beard burn all over her face and neck. Afraid to check the rest of her body, she undressed in the dark and slipped into a long-sleeved nightgown.

Her last thought before sleep took her was not of her husband, but of Boyd. It was Boyd's face in her mind, his kiss on her lips, his hands on her body. The two Paulas stood face to face, and the new Paula was gaining ground.

The telephone rang early Saturday morning, and Paula heard the machine pick up. Still groggy from her late night, she ignored it and rolled over to catch another hour of sleep. But she heard Emma's voice.

"Mom, if you're there, pick up. Mom? Okay, I know you must be there, so I'll give you time to get to the telephone. Mom. Mom, please pick up."

Knowing she'd been bested, Paula picked up the receiver next to the bed and pretended to be awake. "Good morning, darling. How is everyone?"

"We're fine. I'm concerned about you."

"What for?" Oops, a bit too chipper, perhaps.

"I called you three or four times last night, but you never answered. I called as late as eleven o'clock, and you weren't there. Where were you? Are you all right?"

Paula sat up in bed and looked at the clock. Seven a.m. "Yes, dear, I'm fine. I was here last night. I guess I was so busy with homework I didn't hear the phone ring, and I haven't checked the answering machine. Did you leave a message?"

"No, I kept trying to talk to you."

"I'm sorry we missed each other. What were you calling about?"

"Nothing in particular. I just called to chat, but when you weren't there for such a long time, I started to worry."

Paula sighed. Emma had turned into such a mother hen since Sam died. "Don't worry, sweetheart. I'm a grown-up girl so I can start staying out late. I'm making friends with my classmates, and they invite me out from time to time. You know, movies, dinner, just girl stuff. It's sweet that you check in on me, but please don't worry."

She was making it up as she went along, but she thought it sounded pretty convincing. Apparently it satisfied her daughter.

"Well, okay, but be careful. Without Dad here to take care of you, I'm concerned, that's all. You know how we relied on him."

"Yes, we certainly did, but I'm learning to rely on myself now. I didn't mean to worry you. Can we catch up later?"

"Sure. Call me when you're ready to pick up the kids."

Kids? Oh, dear. Today was picnic day at Bluebell Canyon. She had promised Ben and Chloe. She scrambled out of bed. "Oh, right. I'll be over about ten. See you then."

She hung up the telephone and dashed for the shower. She hoped there were no telltale marks on her skin to evidence last night's lovemaking. It would be difficult to explain to the children but impossible to explain to Emma. Long sleeves and a turtle neck should take care of any love bites or residual beard burn.

But the memory of last night was written across her forehead in great red letters. As she soaped Boyd's scent from her body, she was unable to erase the smile from her face.

CHAPTER FIFTEEN

Boyd had finished his shower and was whipping up a Denver omelet in the kitchen of his apartment, whistling a non-tune that expressed his general enthusiasm. It was a beautiful day, one like no other before. Energy flowed. He couldn't sleep, nor could he sit still. He was happy.

Paula's taste remained on his tongue, and his body tightened at the memory of their coupling. He remembered how the firelight had played on the red of her hair, the pink of her sweater, the ivory of her skin, and he was lost.

As a bachelor, he had enjoyed the perks that came with being single. Women were plentiful and eager; he had sampled more than a few. But this time was different. He would need to move carefully. He couldn't seem to get enough of Paula and was overwhelmed with the desire to take care of her. The sound of her voice stirred his senses. He wasn't sure what it all meant, but he wasn't going to question the feeling.

While the coffee brewed, he rang her number, but no one answered. He listened to her voice on the answering machine, then left an enigmatic message. *"I hope you're still sleeping. Recuperating perhaps. I know we got it right the first time, but I'd like more practice, if you please. And I have some other ideas. Call me."*

He returned to the kitchen, and as he relaxed over breakfast, a sense of peace came over him. She didn't call, but he wasn't worried. He would give her time to adjust and acclimate to the new phase of their relationship. He intuitively understood her reluctance and would give her a wide berth, let her set the parameters for the relationship. If it moved forward by increments, he was content.

Last night might have seemed like a huge breakthrough at the time, but she could be experiencing second thoughts. Give her time. He could wait.

****

At the lab on Monday, Paula enjoyed a second cup of coffee while she tried to sort out conflicting emotions. Lovemaking with Boyd had awakened emotions she hadn't felt in a long time and some she had never experienced. And his attitude toward women was new to her. And not a little confusing. Outside the cubicle the phone rang. A moment later, Barry tapped her shoulder and handed her the cordless phone.

"This is a call I think you should take. It's from a Mr. Riley at Michner and Michner, something about the interim financing."

"Interim financing?"

He kept one hand over the mouthpiece. "Don't you remember? The money that will tide us over until the grants come in."

Reluctantly, she took the cordless from him. "What do I know about financing?" Barry shook his head, then walked back to his lab table.

Mr. Riley got right to the point. "I'm checking a few details on the interim financing we provided to your husband's lab operation. As you know, we're only one of the sources for the bridge financing of the lab. We have a shareholders meeting coming up shortly, so we're just getting our ducks in a row."

"Of course," she responded as if she knew all about the operation, although Boyd hadn't explained anything to her in detail. "What specifically do you need verified?"

"The amount of the grant applications, the date for when you anticipate the money coming through. I wasn't the one who negotiated with Professor Mackenzie; it's just been passed to my desk before being delivered to the Board of Directors. Oh, and I need to discuss the APR. I don't see that it's locked in."

Out of her depth, Paula needed to end the call as quickly as possible before she revealed just how little she knew about the financing of the lab. "I believe the best person to give you that information would be Professor Mackenzie himself. I'm basically the hired help, in a manner of speaking. Shall I ask him to call you?"

"I would appreciate that. Thank you, Mrs. Wincott. It's been a pleasure speaking with you."

After she hung up the phone, Paula walked to where Barry worked at an unidentifiable piece of equipment. "Barry, do you know if Professor Mackenzie borrowed money to keep the lab open until we get the grants?"

He glanced at her and continued his work. "I don't. Why?"

"I was under the impression the equipment was donated from manufacturers. Free and clear, as a gift."

"I think that's so," he agreed. "But we also got cash money to pay our salaries. That might have been a loan." He grinned. "Don't worry. We'll be able to pay it all back, with interest, when the grants come through. Dr. Wincott's work is going to bring us worldwide recognition. We'll be famous."

"Of course you will. I have every confidence." She patted his back, then returned to her cubicle to finish sorting paper work.

There was little time to contemplate her relationship with Boyd. Although he called frequently, she held him at a distance, not indulging in romantic conversations, meeting him only for a quick cup of coffee, and then only in a public place. She had worked through the guilt she felt about their lovemaking, but that didn't automatically open the floodgates for future sexual encounters.

An afternoon family visit took on a fresh dimension when Emma noted her mother's new manner. They were having coffee in Paula's kitchen when Emma asked abruptly, "Mom, do you realize you're singing?"

Paula stopped slathering peanut butter on bread and looked at her daughter. "What do you mean, *singing*?"

Emma shrugged. "Well, not exactly singing; but you're humming. And you've been humming a lot lately. Ben even noticed it. He asked me why Nana sings."

"Oh, my goodness, I didn't know I was humming," Paula admitted. "I guess I'm just happy to see my family. You know, I love it when you and children come to visit."

"You never used to hum when we visited. And you look different lately. If I didn't know you, I'd say you're almost glowing. What's going on?"

Turning her back, she continued making the sandwiches. "You know school has turned out to be a tonic for me. I was in such a state after your father passed, and I really needed something to boost my morale. I've made a few friends at school, and I've gotten out a little bit. Maybe that's what you're seeing." She hoped that would settle it.

"I don't know why school would be such an energizer. I found it bloody hard work. Too much work for too little reward, I say." She opened the refrigerator door and took out a carton of milk. "And, you've been to a couple of dances. I think the department has been asking way too much of you. You don't owe them anything, you know."

Paula cut the sandwiches and put them on saucers. "I don't think you understand," she stated without equivocation. "I thoroughly enjoyed those dances. I'm grateful Ed and Helen invited me and wish I had attended the dances in the years before your father died. Maybe that's why I'm humming and why I'm glowing." She added under her breath, "If I'm glowing."

Emma reached into the cupboard for glasses. "Well, I must say I'm surprised. What would Dad think?"

"I don't know," Paula responded, ending the conversation, "but I don't think he would approve." She turned to the kitchen door and called, "Ben, Chloe, lunch."

For once, Emma had no ready comeback.

****

A couple of weeks later, Paula stopped in to see how Barry and the other students were faring. He was happy to see her and gave her a warm greeting. "We missed you. How're classes?

"I'm taking two courses that I enjoy, so I'm feeling elated." She hung her coat on the coat rack and poured herself half a cup of tepid coffee. "Everyone looks busy at the new equipment. How's the research going?"

He took the coffee from her and put it in the microwave. "Uh, well, there's something I wanted to talk to you about. I don't know quite how to tell you."

He waited until the microwave beeped, handed the hot coffee to Paula, and offered her a stool next to his. "I know you've been collecting all the lab notes and organizing them into binders, and it's really been helpful. In fact, it's made everything logical and sequential, and all the pertinent information easy to find. That's the problem."

A prickling sense of unease spread over the nape of her neck. She had expected good news, perhaps even exciting news. "How could that be a problem?"

After a moment, he said, "A piece of the study has gone missing. The work was completed and notated, but the particular piece of notation is missing. We don't know if it was lost after being filed or was never filed at all. In all the mess we had back in that cube, it could have dropped on the floor and been swept up. Bottom line is that we can't find it."

"That doesn't sound like such a catastrophe," she said, relieved that it wasn't something life threatening. "Can't you follow the sequencing and recreate the experiment? I can't believe it's such an impossible task."

He clasped his hands on the workbench and nodded. "I'm afraid it is. Dr. Wincott worked alone in the lab a lot before his retirement, as I'm sure you know. He came in after hours and worked late lots of times, but he was meticulous about writing down every tiny piece of a procedure. The real problem here is that the work was done by Dr. Wincott himself, and we can't duplicate it because... we don't really know what it was."

She was unclear. "Do you there's an information gap that keeps you from proceeding?"

"We can proceed. We're already past that point, and we're moving ahead with the work. But we don't know how he got from A to B. We know he got there because we're already at point E and still moving."

"Do you have to know the link from A to B? If the work is still continuing—"

"We can't write what we don't know. And in the sciences you have to have all the t's crossed." He spread his hands on the workbench in a gesture of frustration. "And we don't."

"Is this something you just discovered? How could you not have known?"

He looked chagrined. "It's our own fault. We've been so busy we haven't kept up with the note sequencing. After you cleaned up the mess and filed everything in chronological order in the notebooks, I started going through them, in preparation for publishing."

Holding back a scream of frustration, she gritted her teeth. "But if you can't publish, Sam's work will never see the light of day. No one will ever know what he accomplished. No, this is not good enough." She refused to accept what he'd told her. "This is the whole purpose for the grants—so that Sam's work would continue, so that he would receive the recognition he deserved. No, no, no! This is not acceptable."

He rubbed his temple. "I'm checking every piece of paper we have, and I'm calling up students who worked with Dr. Wincott over the few years before he retired. Maybe one of them might have a suggestion."

Paula's agitation mounted. "Some of those students have already graduated and moved on. How will you find them?"

Barry heaved a heavy sigh. "Amy Billings worked with him as closely as I. I'm hoping she might know something. I'm even asking for help from the other inorganic professors who might have some idea. Maybe Dr. Wincott said something, anything, to one of them that might give us a clue. I'm not giving up."

Paula couldn't let him do it all. "Let me help. I'll take a binder home every day and pore over it. Just tell me what to look for."

"We've already looked through all the binders, checked every corner of the lab. Would you take a good look in your house? Dr. Wincott might have taken something home with him. Maybe something left in his briefcase or stuck in a book somewhere."

In the few years before his death, Sam became increasingly more suspicious so it was possible he would have hidden a critical piece of work. But where? Could it be somewhere in the house? It wasn't like him to take lab notes home, but he had changed in many ways during those few years.

"How many pages am I looking for? How will I know when I've found it?"

"Let me show you." He took her to the shelves where the notebooks were now stored. Opening one, he searched through until he found the pages he was looking for.

"The missing pages fall between these two dates, in the spring of last year, just before he retired. I know he was working hard in that time period and spent a lot of late nights in the lab. It's as though he leaped across the Grand Canyon and landed safely on the other side."

"Yes," she decided. "I'll do that tonight. I'll call you if I find anything." She grabbed her coat and headed out the door. "And you call me if you come across it."

Before he could respond, she was out the door, heading for the chemistry department office. Lottie was on the telephone as she entered.

"Is Dr. King in?"

Lottie waved her to the adjacent office. Paula saw Ed through the glass pane in the door and gave it a light tap.

He called out, "Come in."

She opened the door and stood on the threshold. "Ed, I need your help."

He removed his reading glasses and gave her his attention. "Paula, you look as if you've seen a ghost. What's wrong?" He rose from his desk and escorted her to a chair. "Are you all right?"

She sat before her knees gave out. "Barry Connors just told me a crucial piece of sequencing is missing from Sam's lab notes and that his work can't be published without it. That can't be true. It can't be possible."

"Hold on, Paula. You're way ahead of me." He closed the door to his office before returning to his desk. "What are you talking about?"

She explained the conversation with Barry and ended with a helpless "What can we do?"

Concern filled his voice. "Let me think this through." He sat back in his chair and slowly shook his head. "Yes, it's true that without the connection between A and B, there's no way to validate the process. But, knowing Sam, I can't believe he didn't write it down very precisely. He bordered on anal retentive, an essential characteristic for a scientist."

"I know he would have written it down," she agreed. "It's just a matter of finding it. I'm going to turn the house upside down. Barry will do the same with the lab. I know it'll turn up." Her voice rose with the level of her anxiety. "It has to turn up."

"I'm sure it will," he soothed.

But Ed didn't feel as certain as he had made himself sound with Paula. Toward the end, Sam had begun to have lapses of memory, forgetting where he had put things, forgetting to log each detail of his lab work. It was possible the missing link would never be found. But Ed didn't want to cause Paula any further alarm, so kept his concerns to himself.

"That's an excellent idea, Paula. I think you're taking the right tack. Sam may very well have carried the paperwork home with him in a briefcase and forgotten to take it back to the lab. And Barry is an exceptionally responsible young man. If it's in the lab, he'll find it."

Only mildly assured, she had hoped Ed would have a ready solution, one that would not rely on chance. She looked to him as she had looked to Sam, as a father figure, the problem solver, the fountain of all wisdom. She was surprised and disappointed that he was none of these. He was a fine man and a credit to the department, but he was not the answer man she sought. She thanked him for his time and left, not feeling any more confident than when she had left Barry.

She would find that paperwork. She had to find it.

CHAPTER SIXTEEN

The next morning, Paula was up early. Overwhelmed by the magnitude of the impending disaster, she couldn't find a beginning point. She sat at the kitchen table, hoping against hope that the papers would suddenly turn up at the lab. When telephone rang, she grabbed it, thinking it would be Barry with good news.

It was Boyd, his voice husky and eager. "I've been hoping you'd call me, but I couldn't wait. I wanted to say... I don't know what I wanted to say exactly. The truth is I just wanted to hear your voice."

"Oh, Boyd," she whimpered. "I've had the most awful news, and I'm at my wits' end. Some of Sam's work is missing."

She told him about her conversation with Barry and also with Ed, the locked desk, the location of the keys unknown. Her stress level had spiraled upwards, and at last she broke. Tears brimmed in her eyes, and her voice quavered. "I don't know what we'll do if we can't find that work."

His response was immediate. "I'm on my way, sweetheart. Just wait for me to look for the keys. And don't worry."

She hung up the phone with a mixture of relief and unease. She wasn't sure she wanted to see Boyd right now, but he was coming to her rescue when she really needed someone. Relief outweighed unease, and she awaited his arrival with gratitude.

Within minutes he was at her door, gathering her up in his arms and allowing her to vent her frustrations. He tucked her head under his chin and held her, stroking her hair and slowly calming her. His reaction to her conversations with Barry and Ed was quiet assurance.

"The important thing is not to worry about the loss of the work. We'll find it. Now, where would be the most logical place for Sam to store his day-to-day notations?"

Uncertain, she shook her head. "His desk, I guess, but when I checked it last evening, it was locked. The only place the key to the desk could be is in the attic where all the boxes of his keys are stored. At least I think that's where they are. I really don't remember."

"Then the first thing is to search for the key. Show me to the attic, and let's get started."

She took him to the trapdoor in the ceiling and pulled down the stairs. He turned to her before starting up. "Go put on a pot of coffee, and I'll start looking for the right box. Did you mark what was in each box when you put them away?"

She thought for a moment. "I don't remember. But, yes, I'm sure I must have. Emma and Wesley helped me packed everything, and Emma is a stickler for detail, just like her father. So, yes, I'm sure we marked each box."

He wanted her to have something to occupy her hands and her mind, something to keep her from breaking down. "I'll find the right box and bring it downstairs. You have the coffee ready."

By the time the coffee was ready, Boyd came into the kitchen carrying a large dusty box. He put it on the kitchen table, wiped it down with a dishcloth, and started pulling off the packing tape.

"Does this look like the right box? It lists a bunch of things, including 'unknown keys' and 'padlocks.'"

Paula recognized Emma's square printing. "Yes,

that's got to be the right one."

She poured two mugs of hot coffee and set them on the table beside the box. The contents were unfamiliar, just a bunch of assorted desk accessories. She dug through compact disk files, boxes of laser labels, electric staplers, three-hole punches, and cellophane-tape dispensers until she located two key rings, both with a jumble of keys. She handed one ring to Boyd. She kept the other, and they began trying each key in the three locks on the desk drawers.

When at last they had the desk open, they searched meticulously. Everything was in its place, but they located nothing resembling the missing documents. She found the correct key and opened Sam's briefcase, but she came up empty again. The briefcase contained nothing, not even a single piece of paper.

Boyd looked around the room. "All right, so this wasn't it. Where else might he have filed his notes, do you think? Other places in the house?"

Defeated, Paula said, "I honestly don't know. His desk is the logical place. That's where he has all of his files that he brought home. The rest are in a series of file cabinets at the lab, but the kids are looking through those. If they find anything, Barry will call so I can stop hunting here. I can't believe this has happened. Is happening. Whatever. After all our hard work." Tears welled again. She wiped her eyes with the back of her hand. "This wouldn't have happened if he hadn't been forced to retire. He'd still be alive and running the lab himself."

Boyd sat on the edge of the desk and pulled her into his arms. "Shh, it's going to be all right, sweetheart. We'll find the notes, don't worry. If they exist, and of course they do, then we'll find them." He laid her head against his chest and smoothed her hair. "They're probably in the notebooks at the lab, and they just got misfiled. I'll bet they've been there all the time. Let's just see what Barry and the kids turn up."

She relaxed against his chest and let him pacify her. It was so good to let someone else help her. She had grown so much since Sam's death and had taken on many new responsibilities. Still, it felt wonderful to have a shoulder to lean on in a time of stress. There was nothing amorous in his embrace. He held her like a friend consoling another friend, and she was grateful.

When she had calmed, they sat at the kitchen table and talked of nothing in particular. He kept her talking just to draw her attention away from the lost documents. He made no reference to their lovemaking, and he made no move to suggest that they were in a closer relationship. At last, when she was in a lighter state of mind, believing the paperwork would turn up, he made a show of looking at his watch.

"I didn't realize it was so late. Sorry to run out on you, but I have an appointment. Shall I come back later?"

She shook her head. "No, not necessary. I'm fine now, thanks." She took his jacket and held it open for him to slide his arms through the sleeves. "I really appreciate your coming over, Boyd. I'm sorry it was for nothing."

He turned to her after zipping the jacket. "Oh, it wasn't for nothing." He gave her a long, slow smile that tugged at something near her heart. "I got to see you, and that was definitely something." He opened the front door and started out.

She touched his arm ever so lightly. "Who is Jocelyn?"

He glanced over one shoulder, looking surprised at the question. "Don't you remember? She's the tall blonde I introduced you to at the Thanksgiving dinner dance last fall."

He knew what she was asking but wanted to make her work for it. Overjoyed that she would ask the question, he dangled a bit of bait. "Silver dress. Jocelyn Sanders."

She bit the hook. "Yes, of course I remember her." How could she forget? "I'm asking who she is to you. Not that it's important. I was just wondering." She caught the grin he tried to hide. "Oh, never mind, it's really not important."

She shoved him through the door, but before she could close it, he stopped halfway, leaned toward her. "She's my sister-in-law. My brother's devoted wife. And she can't hold a candle to you."

He placed a quick kiss on the top of her head and left.

She watched him get into his car. As he pulled away from the curb, she recognized the station wagon approaching and had to think quickly. She hurried back to the kitchen and made herself busy.

Within minutes Emma's face appeared at the kitchen door. "Mom, are you there?"

Chloe and Ben tapped at the glass door, and Abner, their golden retriever, waved his tail and scratched on the wood panels. After Paula opened the door, they all spilled into the kitchen, noise and motion at full momentum. Abner immediately begged for his customary treat while Emma helped Chloe remove her coat. Ben was already at the toy box Paula kept especially for the children.

Chloe's, cheeks ruddy with the cold, had a smile like sunlight. "Hungwy, Nana. Want cocoa."

She knelt to hug the child. "Well, that's just fine, my Chloe. I was just about to make hot cocoa 'cuz I thought my little love babies might be stopping by."

Paula was thankful to have a distraction, but Emma was too quick. "Who was that I saw leaving just now?"

Paula didn't answer right away. She opened the refrigerator and took out milk and vanilla. Emma removed her coat and hung it in the hall. Ben had turned on the television, and very loud cartoons had him occupied.

Emma returned to the kitchen where Paula was pouring milk into a saucepan and mixing cocoa powder and sugar. "Mom? Did you hear what I said?"

Paula kept working but threw a quick response over her shoulder. "Shall I make enough cocoa for you too?"

"That would hit the spot. I'll get the marshmallows." A pause fell before Emma tried again. "Mom, I asked you who was that I saw leaving just now. It was a hot sports car, but I couldn't see who was driving, and we certainly don't know anyone who drives a car like that."

"No, dear, we certainly don't."

"Who was it?"

Paula kept stirring. "Oh, that was just one of your dad's colleagues."

Not to be deflected, Emma opened the pantry and took out a cellophane bag of marshmallows. "That's odd. Why would any of Dad's colleagues come here? You don't know any of them. Do you?"

Paula kept her response nonchalant. "Oh, I've met a few. Of course I've known Ed and Helen for years. You remember they came over for holiday dinners from time to time. And I met a couple of young professors at the Thanksgiving dinner dance. Biochemists, I think. They were quite charming. And there's Professor Shilcroft."

"Mom, be serious. Professor Shilcroft is about a thousand years old. He wouldn't be driving a fancy sports car." She plopped fat marshmallows into mugs and put them near the stove for Paula to pour the cocoa.

Paula forced a laugh. "Well now, I didn't say it was Professor Shilcroft. I only said I know some of the other chemistry professors." She took the cocoa from the stove and stirred vanilla into the mixture, hoping the subject was closed.

"So who was he, Mom? You still haven't answered my original question. And what was he doing here?"

Perhaps a tiny white lie would suffice. "He was delivering some of your dad's paperwork from the lab. I think Barry said their fax was down, so he sent them over with one of the professors."

"Oh. Well. That was nice of him to bring them over."

Relieved, Paula poured cocoa into two mugs and put them on the table. She filled a child-proof cup and handed it to Chloe, who sat at the table in a booster chair. She placed a plate of shortbread cookies in front of Chloe and sat down at the table.

"So, who was it that brought them over?"

God, that girl was tenacious.

"Oh, I'm not sure he gave me his name." Even Paula knew that was weak.

"Surely he introduced himself when he handed you the paperwork," Emma harrumphed.

The feathers were about to hit the fan, but Paula tried one more small evasion. "I believe his name was MacIntosh... or McInnes, I didn't catch it exactly."

Emma's eyes popped. "Mackenzie? Was it Professor Boyd Mackenzie? Dad said he drove a sports car. He always said it was an embarrassment to the department that a man of his age and profession should drive what is commonly called a *chick magnet*. Was it Boyd Mackenzie, Mom?"

Paula knew when she was in a corner, and there was no way out but the truth. "Yes, I believe so." She caught a quick breath and continued with the whole truth. "Actually, Emma, he was here to help me find some of your dad's lost paperwork, experiments that are crucial to the publication of his work. I thought it was very kind of him, especially given their history."

Emma tried to interrupt, but Paula steamrolled her. "As you know, there are plans to publish your dad's latest work; I've already told you about that. What I didn't tell you is that Ed King maneuvered Boyd Mackenzie into writing grant proposals because he's so good at getting funding, so he's been working with Barry Connors to get up to speed. He's been very gracious and extremely helpful."

"Why would Professor Mackenzie agree to do anything to help Dad? They hated each other. Dad talked about it all the time." Emma peered at Paula. "There's something very fishy here. What's going on?"

"Oh, honey, I don't know. When Ed first approached him, he really didn't want to do it, but Ed coerced him into it, so he agreed. Maybe to stay on good terms with Ed. You know, departmental politics and such."

"Or maybe to sabotage Dad's work," Emma concluded, her eyes shouting a great Aha! "No maybe about it. How better to get the upper hand on Dad than to beat him after he died and can't defend himself? Ruin his work and you ruin his reputation. Really, Mom, I can't believe you let him in the house."

Cold water splashed through Paula's veins.

"Emma," she sputtered. "What are you saying? You think Boyd would deliberately try to discredit your dad for some personal gain? Do you think he's in competition with a dead man?"

The idea was repugnant but not far fetched.

"Don't you remember all the stories Dad used to tell us about how Professor Mackenzie tried to undermine his position, how much animosity he showed to Dad, how he wanted to be the star of the department at Dad's expense? You must remember how he treated Dad. You heard it a thousand times."

Emma stopped short. "Did you just call him Boyd?"

Paula faltered, "Did I? Oh, well, yes, I guess I did. We've been working together on the prospectus, and he insisted I use his Christian name, despite my protests. It doesn't mean anything."

Her brain raced. Could he have gulled her with his charm, his apparently superficial charm, into allowing him access to Sam's files? It couldn't be true, but Emma's reasoning made sense— devastating sense.

Emma narrowed her gaze and questioned, "What was he really doing here, Mom? That's the question."

Paula felt like a butterfly pinned to a piece of velvet. Her world fell apart. She laid her face in her hand and wished she could disappear. She might as well unburden herself because it couldn't get any worse. "I think I may have made a serious mistake."

She explained the working relationship with Boyd and the missing papers, leaving out the personal relationship that had evolved. She was deeply embarrassed at how easily she had succumbed to his blandishments.

When she completed the truncated explanation, Emma shook her head slowly. "Oh, Mom, this is terrible. Let me ask you one thing. Did Professor Mackenzie have access to Dad's lab?"

"Why, of course. He was in and out of the lab all the time. He and Barry had to have conversations so Barry could explain your dad's work. It was essential to the grant request."

She tap danced to avoid the obvious conclusion. "But he's a biochemist. He wouldn't know what part of inorganic experiments would be most crucial."

"Unless Barry told him," Emma reminded her.

"Yes," she conceded at last, feeling the ax fall on her neck. "Unless Barry told him. Innocently, of course. They were on the same team, so of course Barry would tell him. He needed to know for the grant request."

"So, of all the people who were in and out of the lab, who would have the best reason to lose those notes? Not Barry, nor any of the other grad students. Not you and certainly not Dad. That leaves the great Boyd Mackenzie, envious of Sam Wincott even now. Oh, Mom, he's hoodwinked everyone, don't you see? Dad was right about him all along, and he's made fools of us."

In spite of the evidence, Paula didn't want to believe it. A shock wave shot through her, and she was too stunned to be angry. "No, darling, he's made a fool of me." She felt gutted. "And there's no fool like an old one," she mumbled under her breath, feeling the weight of her years bearing down on her like lead weights.

"What did you say?"

"I said you're right. I feel like a fool. I believed he was sincere in helping bring your dad's work to fruition."

And she had so wanted to believe in that sincerity.

Emma reached across the table to give her hand a squeeze. "Don't blame yourself. From what Dad said, this man is a consummate liar who could charm the world into thinking he's sent from Heaven. It's as obvious as the nose on your face that he took Dad's papers. The problem is how to get them back. We can't let all of this work go unrewarded and unrecognized. Damn him for a liar and a thief!"

It was obvious who took the notes. How could

she have been so blind to the truth staring her in the face? He was worse than a liar and a thief.

And she had allowed him to make love to her.

No, that wasn't strictly true. She had made love with him as a willing partner, eagerly participating in what was ultimately an act of supreme disloyalty. The profundity of her mistake hit her like a locomotive, and she felt deep, unmitigated shame.

Emma broke the silence. "So where do we go from here? Can anyone in the lab reconstruct Dad's notes?"

"No," Paula sighed. "That's just the problem. The sequencing was done by your Dad alone, and, without the notes, no one can figure out just how he got his results. Without his notations, it's worthless. I don't know what to do. It's not as if we can call the police and report missing lab notes."

As if she'd been struck, Emma sat bolt upright. "Why can't we do exactly that? We could tell them who stole the notes and insist they search his house."

"Emma, they won't take our word that Boyd Mackenzie stole the notes. Lots of people had access. And besides, he's not stupid. He would have destroyed them by now. And we can't prove he had a motive. His cover story is that he admired and respected your dad; he swears he didn't know there was any bad blood between them. I can tell you, he's a master of deception, and he appears completely innocent and cooperative on the surface. We're helpless."

She pounded both fists on the table. "Why was I so gullible, Emma? I hate myself."

Chloe, startled by the pounding, began to wail. Emma gathered her up in her arms and wiped cookie crumbs from her mouth. "We can talk about this later, Mom. I'll take the kids home and talk to Wesley. Maybe he'll have some ideas." She yelled into the living room, "Ben, turn off the TV and get your jacket. We're going home. Come and say good-bye to Nana."

Ben ran into the kitchen with his usual full speed. "Hey Nana, what's this?"

CHAPTER SEVENTEEN

He waved a scrap of silk and lace in the air. Paula's torn panties! She had to move fast to distract him. And Emma.

"That's my pretty underwear, darling. I must have misplaced it when I was putting away the laundry."

She reached out to take it from the boy, but Emma got to him first. "What were you doing in Nana's bedroom, Ben?" She took the fragment of silk panty and started to hand it to Paula.

"I wasn't in Nana's bedroom. I found it under the sofa by the fireplace."

Emma stopped short and took a closer look at the wisp in her hand. Understanding dawned slowly but with torrential force. "Mom, this wasn't in the laundry. And it's been ripped to pieces—as if someone tore it off someone."

The riveting gaze made Paula's heart sink. "You had sex!" The accusation rang with the force of an earthquake.

A long silence fell while Emma sputtered and Paula cast about for an explanation that didn't involve the truth. At the look of surprise on Ben's face, Paula said gently, "Take your sister to the toy box and see what you can find for her, sweetheart." She ushered the children out of the room before their mother erupted again.

"You've had sex! Don't even try to deny it!" Emma raged. "I can't believe what I'm seeing, but there's no other explanation. My mother, the grandmother of my children, my father's widow. He's

146

not even cold in the ground, and you can't wait to take a lover!"

"Your father has been dead for more than a year, Emma," Paula corrected without emotion. "I've been alone that long."

"What do you mean *alone*? You have a family. You have memories of a wonderful life with a wonderful man. How can you say you're alone?"

"You have Wesley and the children. I don't even have a pet. I come home to an empty house every night. And I haven't taken a lover."

"What would you call it when someone tears your panties off, then throws them under the sofa? What were you doing if you weren't having sex?"

"It happened. It wasn't planned. I don't have a lover," Paula answered dully. "I don't even have a friend."

It was true. She had made a profound mistake in Boyd Mackenzie. He had pretended to be her friend, and she had been duped.

Emma was not to be deterred. "Mom, you're fifty years old. You're past that kind of kinky sex. I can't imagine Dad ever behaved like that." She placed both hands over her eyes. "My God, I don't even want to think about this."

Unable to defend herself against her daughter's onslaught, Paula writhed in shame. "I'm sorry. I've made a fool of myself in more ways than one. I've let the family down, and—"

"Who is he?"

Paula started. "What?"

"Who is this degenerate?"

Alarms clanged. Several stories ran through her truth filters. At last she decided evasion was the best response. "It's not important. It won't happen again. It's no one you would know."

"You're not the kind of woman who would do something like this. He must have taken advantage of you. Is that it? He forced you, didn't he? You've been raped! We should call the police."

Paula caught Emma's hand before she reached the phone. "No! I wasn't raped. I wasn't forced in any way. It was a mistake; let's leave it at that. I allowed it, and I won't allow it again. Just drop it."

Emma gave her a damning look that touched her to the core, then twisted. "I can't believe you were a willing participant. It's just not like you. It's not the mother I've always known."

"That's because you've never known me as anything but your mother, so how can you know what my personal life is like?" She put her hand up to stop Emma before she could speak again. "No! We can talk about this another time. Right now we have something more important to deal with. We have to find your father's papers. You're going to ask Wesley if he has any ideas."

Her daughter's face was a picture of conflicting emotions, but Paula's appeal to priorities caught her in mid-rant. "All right, we'll let it go for now. But we'll have to talk about it sometime."

"When the time is right," Paula answered. She called to the children, "Ben, Chloe, come. You're going home."

Emma gathered up coats and herded the children out without another word to her mother.

****

Her life in pieces, and in a pit of depression, Paula barely recognized that Emma and the children left.

Later that evening, Wesley, in full protective mode, called. One of his most endearing traits was his eagerness to step up to the plate when any of his family needed help. He was a warrior in horn-rimmed glasses, but a warrior nonetheless, and she loved him for it.

"Emma just told me what happened at Sam's

lab, and I want you to take it easy and not get yourself in a state," he said. "I have a friend who's a detective with the Boulder police. I'm sure he can conduct an investigation that won't bring a lot of publicity to the department or the university."

Obviously Emma hadn't shared the panties episode with Wesley, and for that Paula was grateful. However, she was only a little calmed by Wes's idea. She had to protect the reputation of CU and the Chemistry Department, and she absolutely could not risk newspaper or television coverage, especially if the investigation yielded nothing.

"Thanks, darling, I really appreciate your help. I guess we have to circle the wagons, don't we?"

"You bet we do. Nobody messes with my girl and gets away with it. This is a matter of family honor."

"But Wes, how can your friend conduct an investigation without interviewing people and without anyone getting wind of what's happened? This could completely jeopardize Sam's funding, and Barry would have to close down the lab. You understand, don't you? It has to be very discreet."

"Don't worry. My friend is a detective, not a uniformed officer. It's his job to fly under the radar. Let me talk to him at least. We're working in the dark without any knowledge of how to proceed, so it seems like a good idea to ask someone in the profession, don't you agree?"

"Of course I agree, reluctantly. I'm still in shock about the whole thing, so I need a little time to assimilate the information. Then I want to put that bastard in jail where he belongs." She thought for a moment. "How much time do we have?"

Wesley was adamant. "We don't have any time. Didn't you say Sam's funding is pending? What if this guy didn't even write the proposal? Did you consider maybe he just told you he was writing it so he could gain access to Sam's lab? Did you think of that?"

Oh God. That couldn't be. She hadn't considered that possibility, but it made complete sense. Pretend to Ed King that he was reluctant and allow himself to be coaxed into the catbird seat. Coaxed into making love to her. No, she had made love. Boyd had simply had sex with the wife of his enemy—the final victory over a dead man. Her devastation was complete. Now she understood the depths of despair.

She sat down, still holding the telephone. "You're right. We don't have time. I don't even know if the proposal was submitted. All I have is Barry's word that Boyd told him he had submitted it. All right, tell your friend to go ahead with the investigation. I'll ask Ed King to get verification that the grant proposal was submitted. If he even knows."

"Okay. I'll get right on it. And don't let this get you down. Remember, you're not alone. We're all in this together. Family first."

He gave her a sense of solidarity, if nothing else, and she managed a faint smile. "Thanks, Wes. I love you."

"Love you, too."

She hung up the phone and sat for a moment, contemplating her next move. Should she allow herself a good weep or gird herself for a battle?

Ah, what the hell. She would have a hot bath, a good cry, and a nap. Then she would think about bringing Boyd to justice.

She didn't know where to turn. She couldn't accuse him outright, nor could she confide in Ed or Lottie or any of the graduate students. They were convinced the sun rose and set on Boyd Mackenzie, and she couldn't prove otherwise. After thinking the situation through, she decided to play ignorant. If he didn't know she suspected him, perhaps he might give himself away. But it would be impossible to continue to see him, knowing the depth of his deception. Fortunately, part of his guilt would become obvious when no grant money was forthcoming.

She stopped by the Chemistry office the next day, hoping to see Ed without making a point of the visit. She was in luck.

He rose from his desk and waved her to come in. "Paula, my dear. Just the lady I was hoping to see. Come in."

Lottie stuck her head around the corner. "Oh, and don't you look lovely. Would you like a cup of tea? I just filled the brown betty."

Paula gratefully accepted tea as an excuse to sit and chat for a while with both Lottie and Ed. He took her coat and hung it on a peg by the door. She took a seat opposite his desk.

"Are you sure you're not busy, Ed? I don't want to take up your time if you're working on lesson plans or something."

"Not at all. I'm teaching graduate seminars this semester, and we just talk in class. So I'm at liberty. How have you been? Helen sends you her best regards."

She took off her gloves and stuffed them into her handbag. "Oh, fine, fine. Busy with my new studies. I must say I was surprised that I learned so much last term. It was less arduous than I had expected, and World Lit was actually great fun. I think I'm going to enjoy being a student."

"I told you it's never too late to learn. These young folks have nothing on their elders, and you'll discover that for yourself as times goes on. I'm sure you'll continue to do very well."

Lottie handed the cup of tea to Paula and set a cup on Ed's desk. She pulled up a seat beside Paula, who fiddled with the tea to cover her nerves. "I saw your name on Professor Sloan's class roster. Are you enjoying his class?"

"We just started, but yes, I think I'll do fine."

She didn't know quite how to segue into her reason for coming except just to jump in. "Ed," she began casually, "How long does it generally take to get an answer after a grant proposal is made? I mean, when would we reasonably expect to hear something about Sam's funding?"

"In my experience it could take three months, six months, sometimes even longer, but I wouldn't worry. You know the lab is fully functional with the interim financing, so they can last as long as it takes for the real money to show up."

"Yes, I know about the interim financing, but I'm embarrassed to say I don't really know how much it was or where it came from, so I can't put it into my bookkeeping ledger to track the expenditure. All of the equipment was just bought and delivered. Do you know anything about where it came from? How much it cost?"

He raised a hand to pooh-pooh her. "Not really, but don't you worry yourself about that. Mackenzie took care of it all, and I have to confess none of us knows any more than you do. But it really doesn't matter. It wasn't a loan. It came from businessmen with whom he has a fine professional relationship. They know him well and trust his judgment, so they were willing to dig into their pockets and contribute to a worthy cause. He's a fine man. We're lucky to have him helping out."

She had to work at not showing her distaste. "Do we have any receipts, anything to indicate the exact date when the papers were submitted? I'd like to put everything together in the files I've set up in the lab."

Ed turned to Lottie. "I think we must have something somewhere, don't we? Take a look around and see if you and rustle that up for Paula. No hurry. It's just a formality."

Lottie acknowledged his request. "Sure thing. I'm sure I have it around my desk somewhere."

Ed returned his attention to Paula. "She'll find it and mail it to you, or maybe the next time you're in the office you can pick it up. Now, as I said, I was hoping to see you. We're going to spend a week up at the cabin during the break, and Helen insists you have to come along. She won't take no for an answer, and my life won't be worth living if I go home tonight without a firm commitment from you. Besides, I'd love to have you join us as well. Please say yes, and solve my problem."

She leaped at the opportunity to get away from her troubles for a week, especially in the company of old friends. And away from Boyd Mackenzie.

"Oh, Ed, I'd just love to come up. Tell Helen I'm very appreciative of the invitation. Just tell me when, and I'll start packing. Shall I bring anything special?"

A wide grin spread across his face. "You, my dear, are the most special thing we could possibly take to our cabin. Just bring your lovely self and whatever book you've been meaning to read. We don't do much else besides read, eat, and talk, maybe go for a walk in the snow—it's like powder up there—and sit by the fire with a hot drink at night. I can tell you one thing: you'll sleep like a baby."

She stood to leave. "What is the travel plan, Ed? Will you give me directions?"

"We'll pick you up on Saturday morning. Since you haven't been there before, I don't want you to get lost in Estes Park. The snow whites out everything this time of the year."

"Sounds good. I'm looking forward to a week away." She waved good-bye to Ed and blew a kiss to Lottie. And missed the look that passed between them.

CHAPTER EIGHTEEN

The drive to Estes Park was beautiful. With the dry, crisp air and bright sun, it was the best of Boulder winter days. No wonder skiers from all over the world came to Colorado in the winter. The snow was clean and white, and the snow tires sounded a satisfying crunch as they made their way up the mountainside. The Kings' cabin was perched near the top of a hill and afforded a panoramic view that included the rosy-gold sunrise on one side and the purple-streaked sunset on the other. Ed had insisted on glass for one whole side of the cabin, and three plump sofas were arranged to focus on the view. A large open fireplace kept the room toasty, and, with a hot buttered rum in her hand, Paula felt the tension flow out through her fingertips. She took Ed's advice and brought a novel for a relaxing read, and she looked forward to doing nothing for a week.

Sunday morning she slept later than usual, a result of the fresh air, she concluded, and enjoyed a breakfast of sausage and waffles. Helen lounged in a hot-pink muumuu and house slippers while Ed went for a walk after his usual coffee and toast.

The hardwood floors were polished to a dark sheen, and Paula noted with satisfaction that no one wore shoes in the house. She wore heavy wool socks that continued to buff the floors with each step, and a thick white fisherman's sweater topped bright yellow sweatpants.

"More waffles? How are your sausages holding out?"

Paula wiped her mouth. "No more, Helen. I'm

stuffed to the gills."

"You've hardly eaten anything. No matter, this mountain air will whet your appetite."

"After that lumberjack breakfast, I'll be fine until dinner."

They sat at the window and indulged in long-overdue girl talk until they heard Ed stamping the snow off his boots outside the door. A blast of frigid air preceded his cheery, "What are you girls up to in here?"

Helen shivered. "Oooh, close that door, honey. It's cold."

"It's brisk winter air. Good for the soul." Ed hung up his parka and took a seat on the sofa next to his wife. "You know, I saw a car heading up the road just now. Looked as if it was going up to Mackenzie's place. Is he up for the break?"

Paula's ears pricked up. Boyd had a cabin near this one?

Helen turned and rested her head against Ed's shoulder. "I don't know, dear. I haven't seen him, but he keeps so much to himself I never know when he's here. Did you recognize the car?"

"I don't think I've ever seen it before, but maybe it's Reid and Jocelyn. They sometimes come up for a week-end when she can get away. Maybe later we'll all take a walk up there and say hello. It would be the neighborly thing to do."

Paula didn't feel like being neighborly, but she kept quiet. There would be too much explaining to do if she made a fuss.

"It could've been some of the other faculty, but it's not like Boyd to socialize up here. We all come to the cabins to get away," Ed continued, leaning back and resting his feet on the coffee table.

Helen stood. "I'm going to have a long hot shower and get dressed. I can't hang about in my dressing gown all day. You and Paula entertain each other for a little while." She leaned down to kiss Ed on the cheek and then disappeared down the hall.

The wheels turned in Paula's head. Who would be visiting Boyd this far away from campus? It wasn't her business, of course, but she couldn't help wondering who would be close enough to him to be invited to his getaway cabin. Did he have a woman? Unreasonably, a lightning streak of jealousy shot through her body.

****

Boyd was stoking the fire when he heard a car drive up outside the cabin. He pulled back the curtain and saw an unfamiliar car in the drive. The woman getting out was equally unfamiliar, but he opened the front door as she walked up the wooden steps.

"Good morning, Professor," she greeted brightly. "Cold up here, isn't it? She offered him a mitten covered hand. "I need to talk to you. May I come in?"

He was puzzled but not unmannerly. She appeared to know him, but he couldn't recall having met her. Maybe one of his new students this term. "Of course, come in out of the cold." He ushered her into the cabin and took her coat. "Stand over by the fire and warm yourself. Can I get you something?"

Standing with her back to him, she took off her mittens and spread her hands toward the fire. "Coffee, you have it," she answered over her shoulder.

He poured a cup of hot coffee from the counter and set it on the coffee table. "I'm sorry to appear oafish, but do I know you?"

She turned and frowned. "It's me, Amy Billings, from the lab. Maybe you don't recognize me all bundled up like this."

He remembered a thin woman with a dark pony tail, but this woman's hair was completely covered with a black knitted cap. However, the face with

156

large dark eyes was consistent with his memory. "Of course. Amy Billings. You're one of Dr. Wincott's grad students." He had a vague recollection of her, but out of her element he hadn't immediately placed her. "What are you doing all the way up here in the middle of winter?"

She slipped off her mukluks and walked in her socks back to the warm hearth. She stood facing away from the fire, hands behind her back to warm them. "I'm sorry to barge in on you like this, but it seemed like the right time. Everything just fell into place, so I came on up. I hope it's all right."

Though his memory of her was remote, he was interested in the reason behind the unexpected visit. "Is there something I can do for you?"

"I just wanted to see you alone, and I knew you had a cabin up here. I heard them talking about it in the office. It was just a matter of finding out which one was yours. But I'm smart."

"Ms. Billings—"

She tilted her head and smiled. "Call me Amy."

"Amy," he amended, still curious. "If you had needed to see me alone, I have office hours posted on my door. You could see me virtually any time. You didn't have to make the long trip all the way up here just to see me alone."

She smiled and shifted her weight slightly. "I think you'll agree this is the right venue for our discussion, once you hear what I have to say." She pulled off her cap, and thick dark hair fell about her shoulders.

Yes, he realized, this was the woman he had spoken with in Sam's lab some weeks ago. But what could she want now? He sat on the arm of the sofa, facing the fire, and leaned toward his visitor. "What is it exactly that we have to talk about? I thought we had concluded our discussions. I've already submitted the grant requests, you know. We're just waiting for responses from the various institutions." His tone was matter of fact, despite the myriad of questions buzzing in his mind.

She glanced around the room with an approving eye. "This is quite a place you have here, Boyd. Very tasteful, very masculine. Who decorated it for you?"

She called him Boyd. Puzzled by the direction of the conversation, he searched her face for a clue, but her expression revealed nothing.

He played for time. Surely she'd get to the point momentarily. "Well, it's not really decorated. I just brought up some things I like, and it works for me." When she gazed at him in rapt silence, he broke the deadlock. "Amy, why exactly are you here?"

"It's very cozy, and it reflects your personality. Do you bring women up here?"

He started at her impertinence. "My private life is not your business. And you haven't answered my question. What do we have to talk about that can't wait until I return to campus next week?"

Unabashed, she twirled her cap in her hands and cast her eyes downward. "Oh, I suppose it could wait. I just thought this would be an ideal location for us to spend some time. You know, we never run into each other on campus, so how would we ever get to know each other?"

Know each other?

"Amy, you'll have to help me out here. I'm still unclear on your motive for coming up here. You and I have a purely professional interest in each other."

She turned large dark eyes to him. "What are you saying? I saw how you looked at me when we were talking about Professor Wincott's work. It was as if you saw right through me, and you knew everything—even how I feel."

Every silent internal alarm went off. This was not the first time he had dealt with a student who wanted more than just an education. He had handled it successfully several times, and would handle it again, even if this one was more inventive than the others. She had tracked him to his hideaway.

"Amy. I respect you as a highly-intelligent chemist and a valued member of Professor Wincott's team, but—"

"You can let that go, Boyd. I know you feel it too. You must. You wouldn't have spent so much time talking with me. And you smiled and told me how much you admired the work I was doing and my dedication to Professor Wincott. You touched my hand, remember? Then your eyes told me you knew how I felt about you, that you understood."

A tiny frown appeared between her brows. "Don't try to pretend. I've come up here because you couldn't invite me without chancing recriminations from administration. But I could come up on my own, so I took the initiative." She raised a hand in reassurance. "Don't worry. No one knows I'm here."

Thunderstruck, he didn't move. This was going to be difficult. He looked at her carefully, trying to determine how delicately to handle her. She looked to be about twenty-eight, difficult to tell because she was so slender and dwarfed by a bulky black sweater. Black eyebrows gave her an intense gaze, her lips were thin. She was not unattractive, but clearly she was not experienced in the nuances of male/female social interaction. He didn't want to be harsh or unkind, nor could he allow her to continue along this vein.

"I'm sure there are many young men your age who would find you very attractive." She responded with a smile, but he continued, "I'm old enough to be your father. You must see that. We just had a couple of meetings about work, that's all. If I misled you in any way, I assure you it was unintentional, and I apologize if you misunderstood."

She crossed quickly to the sofa and flung her arms around him. "How can you deny what's passed between us? You know it, and I know it." Her tone brooked no argument. "You're not too old for me. I'm almost thirty years old. I have my Ph. D, but I turned down job offers so I could continue to work with Professor Wincott. He was an inspiration, and he needed me."

She touched the tip of his chin with her forefinger and pushed gently. "You're just the right age for me. Professor Wincott was eighteen years older than his wife, and their marriage worked out just fine. She was only a kid when they got together. I'm an adult."

She leaned back and looked into his eyes. "She was a silly little girl who offered him nothing. I'm a grown, educated woman, an equal who can work side by side with you."

Her fantasy had gone far enough. Boyd tried tactfully to remove her arms from his neck, but she would not disengage. "Amy, try to understand, what you're asking is impossible. You haven't considered—"

"Listen to me, Boyd. I worked in Professor Wincott's lab for years. I was devoted to him. He was a genius, and I worshiped at his feet. He trusted me, relied on me, asked my opinion. When he worked late, I stayed just to be in his presence and watch him work. I learned everything I know about chemistry from Sam Wincott and will defend his memory no matter what it takes."

Though veering off topic, she caught his attention. He now listened intently. "I know what you and that woman are planning. She didn't deserve him, and now you're going to help her get his work completed and published?"

"It's why we're all working so hard, Amy."

"It's not going to work out the way you planned,"

she said.

She loosened her grip on his neck and leaned away to smile up at him. "A piece of sequencing is missing."

He nodded carefully. "Yes, that's true. I'm sure we'll locate paperwork that fits the puzzle together."

"I don't think so," she said in a child's sing-song tone.

Bewildered, he stared at her. "You want his work published, don't you?"

"Of course I do," she snapped. "I would be the first in line to publish his work, if it were possible." She gave him a sly grin. "But the experiment won't be found. It's gone."

He grasped her elbows to hold her away from him. "What do you mean it won't be found? It must be found, or all of the work was for nothing. Is that what you want?"

She whirled out of his arms. "You don't understand anything, do you?"

She sat on the sofa and buried her head on the arm opposite him. Her voice was anguished as she choked out what he feared hearing. "Don't you see? I checked and rechecked the sequencing, but it didn't work. I must have run the experiment a hundred times, over and over again, but I couldn't make it work."

She sat back up and rubbed her forehead with both hands. "Professor Wincott must have made a mistake. Maybe he wrote it down wrong, I don't know. In those last few years, he wasn't as thorough as he once was. He sometimes missed things, but I was always there to catch them."

She looked up, her eyes bright. "And he really appreciated that. He told me so. He said *I* was his right arm, not *her*, and he didn't know how he would get along without me. He said there were people who wanted him to fail, but I was his only support system."

Eager to keep her talking, Boyd said, "You're a very bright student. I'm sure you were indispensable to him."

"Oh, yes," she agreed. "He said I was indispensable. Anyway, he must have worked on this part by himself, late at night. He sometimes did that, you know, work late alone. I wasn't there for him, and he must have forgotten to write down a step or two because it didn't work. It can't work the way he says it did."

Eyes focused on Boyd, she said deliberately, "I can't let anyone know he made a mistake, you see. He really was brilliant, but he made a little error because I wasn't there to help him."

There it was. Worst-case scenario right in front of him. How would he find the words to tell Paula?

Amy sat up and grasped his hands tightly, as if to convince him. "It's for the best. This way, no one will know, and his reputation will be intact. This is what he would have wanted, I'm sure of it. That woman would have ruined everything. She would've shone the light of failure on him, but I was there for him this time, and I protected him."

"You protected him." He spoke soothingly, telling her what she needed to hear while his mind raced to assimilate what she had just revealed to him.

"In September, when the new professor comes, we'll move in a new direction, and all of this will be forgotten. Isn't that clever?" She offered him an earnest look. "You know, I wasn't in love with Professor Wincott; he was far too old for me. But I admired his mind. He was the wunderkind of his day. But you're the wunderkind now, and you're not too old for me."

She sat back and held out her arms to him. "Everything has a way of working itself out."

He didn't know what to say. "Amy, this is a lot to absorb at one sitting. I need to some time to think this through, to decide the best way to proceed." He tried keeping his voice level. "You've given me so much information, and I really have to consider other's feelings as well."

She came to her feet, began pacing. "What other people? You're talking about *her*, aren't you? It's not enough that she had him, now she has to have you, too. Well, it's not fair. Just tell her you love me and we're going to be together. She can go back to being a widow, or let her find somebody else. You and I belong together. I can help you just like I helped Professor Wincott."

Her rant showed no signs of slowing. "This time it'll be better. You'll see. I brought my suitcase so I can stay here. After we return to Boulder, we'll let everyone think the lab notes are lost. No one needs to know they were destroyed."

Knowing he must tread carefully, he stood, then took her by the shoulders, gently so as not to alarm her. "I see you've thought this through carefully, and I see your logic. But I don't think it's a good idea for you to stay here."

Her bottom lip thrust out in a pout. "Why not?"

He scrambled for a sound reason. "Professor King and his wife have a cabin just down the road. I wouldn't want to damage your reputation if they saw your car in the driveway. Everyone thinks very highly of you, and I wouldn't think of compromising your reputation. You know how people gossip, especially in the university setting. They might think I'd broken the rules by having a physical relationship with a student. It could cost me my position, and I know you wouldn't want that."

While she seemed to consider the import of his words, he added, "My brother and his wife are due to arrive tomorrow, and it could be embarrassing for all of us. You see that, don't you?"

She chewed on her lip for a moment. "I hadn't thought about that. I wouldn't want people to think ill of us. But I really wanted to stay with you."

"I know you did. But can you see why it's not a good idea? Circumstances are against it right now. Why don't you go back to Boulder and continue as normal. I'll be back in a week, and we'll have a long talk then."

"We will?" She sounded like a little girl, not a woman of almost thirty.

"Of course. We'll sort everything out when I get back." He walked her to the door and held her coat for her, then buttoned it up and placed her cap back on her head. "Don't worry about the lab notes. I'll take care of everything."

She bounced down the steps and waved a cheery good-bye. "I'm so glad we had this talk. I know everything is going to work itself out. See you back at your office next week."

She got into her car, then leaned out the window to call, "I love you."

As Amy drove away, Boyd's shoulders slumped while he contemplated this abrupt turn of events. How could he explain to Paula without breaking her heart?

She had come to mean so much to him, he couldn't bear to see her hurt.

He tried to analyze his feelings. Had he hoped to win her by endorsing Sam's work?

Yes.

From the beginning he had wanted to be a hero in her eyes.

A middle-aged hero who could leap tall buildings in a single bound, who could perform the miracle of resurrecting her husband's work, who could protect her from disappointment, who could be everything to her.

It went far beyond physical desire now.

He loved her—with all the passion of his years. But he couldn't tell her.

Perhaps he could never tell her.

CHAPTER NINETEEN

After Paula arrived back home from the mountains, Wesley telephoned with an update. "Good news. My friend has a report that may put Mackenzie where he belongs. It might not get him jail time, but he'll certainly lose his job. The evidence is circumstantial, but it puts a dark cloud of suspicion over his head. His reputation will be ruined, and he won't be able to get another position anywhere in the academic world."

"I thought we were going to wait a week to see if anything turned up," she reminded him. "Does this mean your friend went ahead with the investigation?"

"Only a preliminary foray," he replied. "But everything points to Mackenzie."

"Then we were right; it was Boyd all along."

She wanted justice, not only for Sam, but for herself also. Boyd Mackenzie had betrayed them both with easy charm and smooth manner. Thank God no one knew of their personal relationship, or she would never be able to hold her head up again. She had been suckered, and nothing could wipe the stain from her soul.

So much for trying to forge a new life. Emma had been right. She should quit school, devote herself to her family, and live out her years unproductively as Sam's circumspect widow.

"Do you have some time today so that we could come over and talk with you?" Wesley asked. "Joe would like to get a few more details. It won't take long."

Paula didn't want to see the detective, but she agreed, if only to put the whole sordid episode behind her. "Why don't you bring him by this afternoon?"

It would be distasteful but no more so than the whole squalid mess she had made. Yes, she had made the bed she was now lying in. She could blame no one but herself. The enormity of it appalled and disgusted her.

She was ready when they arrived a few hours later, Wesley with a quick, firm step that indicated he was committed to a swift end to Paula's unease. He introduced his friend, Detective Joseph Peterson, a square young man about Wesley's age, with piercing grey eyes. His no-nonsense manner gave her confidence. He declined her offer of coffee, took the seat she offered, and got right down to business. "All right, Mrs. Wincott, this is what we have." He opened a notebook, flipped through the pages, and nodded when he found the right one. "According to the information Wes provided, this fellow Mackenzie teaches at CU, and had a beef with your late husband. Some kind of academic competition. Is that correct, ma'am?"

Boyd had sworn it wasn't true, that it was all one sided, but now she wasn't sure. She trod lightly. "My husband told us so many times."

He wrote something in the notebook. "So he had motive."

"We feel he did, yes," she answered, hating the words as they fell from her lips.

"Then he had access to your husband's notes, I believe, through the lab?"

"Yes. He met several times with my husband's lab supervisor, Barry Connors, so he was in the lab more than once. I don't know how often actually."

"So if the notes were in the lab, he had opportunity. Now, Mrs. Wincott, suppose the missing notes were not at the lab at all. What if your husband brought them home? This Mackenzie fellow wouldn't have access to your home, with your husband's attitude toward him and all, correct?"

Here it comes.

She hadn't wanted this part made public but felt she had to make a strong case against Boyd. "Detective Peterson, there were two occasions when Professor Mackenzie was physically in this house, ostensibly to help with the funding of my husband's work. I had accepted his help on face value, so I suspected nothing."

The detective turned a quizzical eye to her. "But if Professor Mackenzie and your husband were at such odds, why did he help in any manner? Didn't you question his reasons for coming to your home?"

She loathed having to confess her naiveté, but said, "Of course, but the chairman of the chemistry department had convinced him to write a grant proposal. And Professor Mackenzie swore to me repeatedly there was no animosity on his part toward my husband. He was very convincing, and I wanted to believe him."

Off Detective Peterson's look, she amended quickly, "For the sake of the work, of course."

He clucked and nodded. "Right. So now we have motive and opportunity. Who else had access to those notes?"

"Any number of people, thought no one else had a motive. My husband had devoted students and lifelong friends, all of whom wanted to see his work completed."

"That's true, Joe," Wesley added. "Ask anyone in the department. Sam was highly respected and well loved by students and teachers alike."

"Why don't you cut to the chase and search Professor Mackenzie's house?" she asked. "Isn't that where we're going with this?"

Wes jumped in. "No good, Paula. We couldn't get a search warrant without more substantial evidence, you know, probable cause and all that. Besides, if he took the notes, he would have burned them by now."

"*If* he took them? Wesley, he's the only suspect. Isn't that right, Detective?"

The young man shifted in his seat. "Well, yes, ma'am, but you understand we don't have any hard evidence. This fellow is just the most obvious suspect. And most obvious is not always the perpetrator."

"But you have enough to question him. You just said you have motive and opportunity. You have enough to go to the head of the department with your suspicions."

"We have enough to question him, but you understand we're not going to find those notes. You can consider them gone. And without them, we can't prosecute. It's really an internal problem, something that should be handled by the chemistry department itself. I'm afraid all we can do is cast suspicion, and that might not be completely fair. What if Mackenzie is innocent?"

"Innocent?" Wesley exclaimed. "Joe, he's insinuated himself into my mother-in-law's life for the purpose of stealing a man's life work." He turned to Paula, realization dawning in his face. "Boyd! Wait a minute. That's the rock climber Ben likes so much, isn't he?"

Paula nodded, grim-faced. Her humiliation was complete.

"You see, Joe," Wes exclaimed, "he even managed to charm my six-year-old son. He'll stop at nothing to get his hooks into this family."

Paula felt the heat of shame creep into her cheeks. How much had Wesley told his friend?

Detective Peterson closed his notebook and rose from his seat. "I guess that's all I need for now, Mrs.

Wincott. I'll have a talk with the head of the department, Dr. King, I believe, and get back to you and Wes. I wish there were something more substantial I could offer you. Maybe something will turn up, but in the meantime, let me take it from here. No good turning yourself inside out with worry. If we can't nail him for theft, we can at least shake him up a little."

At the door, Wesley gave Paula a hug and whispered in her ear, "We'll get him one way or the other. He can't treat my family like this and get away with it."

She was relieved when they left. She knew Wesley would leave no stone unturned, and she trusted his friend to do a thorough investigation. But she was not prepared to accept that she had failed Sam.

She had to redeem herself. But how?

CHAPTER TWENTY

The spiral began its ugly journey south. She played the message machine and found a series of calls from Boyd, obviously placed before he knew the police had been alerted.

"I've missed you. All I've done for the last week is think about you. What we shared was amazing, and I know you felt it too. This isn't just some passing fancy. We have something unique, and I won't let it go. Call me."

"I want to see you, need to see you. Call me."

"I need to touch you again, even if it's only for a moment. Call me."

It was out of her hands now. The police would question him, and he would be forced to admit his chicanery.

Then the final call came, after he learned what she had done. Her stomach contracted. Even after all that had happened, the sound of his voice affected her in ways she couldn't fight.

"Paula, I've just had a visit from a Boulder police detective. I thought you and I understood each other, but I see we have some serious communication issues. Please pick up the telephone." He waited a moment, then said, *"Okay, when you get this message, call me. If you don't call me back, I'm coming over, so make up your mind."*

She wouldn't call him, but it didn't matter. He would come. She didn't have long to wait. As dusk fell, a pounding sounded at her door. "Paula, open up. It's Boyd."

He didn't shout, but his voice reverberated

through the house and throughout the recesses of her mind where she tried to hide from him. "I know you're there, so you might as well open the door. I'm not going away until we talk." There was something different in his voice, something she didn't want to hear.

He pounded harder. "Open."

Reluctantly, she unlocked the door. He pushed it open. Even after all she knew about him, he still overwhelmed her senses. The memory of their lovemaking was alive in the look he gave her. And the anger in his voice couldn't conceal his desire for her. His eyes glittered as he spoke in a low, steely voice, barely above a whisper. "When did you decide I'm a thief?"

With the question hanging in the air, he stood in the doorway, making no attempt to enter the room. It was obvious he was trying to hold his temper in check, but a muscle twitched under the beard-stubbled jaw, and his blue eyes held barely-banked fire.

His anger rolled over her, almost tangible in its intensity. How could he take this stance? She was the one who should be angry. But she wasn't. She was profoundly disappointed and bereft. In that moment she realized with surprise and startling clarity that, despite everything, she had fallen in love with Boyd Mackenzie.

Now she had to regain her composure and some semblance of control in order to put him out of her life. Her voice shook, but she held her own. "I didn't make that decision. You did. And you had me fooled until I put all the pieces together. I didn't want to believe it, but I had no choice. All the pieces point to you. What else can I think?"

He stuffed his hands into the pockets of his sheepskin jacket. He spoke softly, but his voice was like flint. "You could believe what I've told you."

She ran a hand through her hair. "That's just the problem. I did believe what you told me. I fell neatly into the plan you devised. Poor, foolish, lonely widow. How easy it was to convince me of everything you wanted me to believe. Your charm is still intact, Professor, and it works on all of the females, young and old."

He turned his head away from her and held up his palm to stop her. "This is the same old song you've sung since I met you. The verses are getting stale. If you can't separate yourself from your role as Sam's gatekeeper, then you're the loser. You're not protecting Sam. You're protecting yourself from life, but I can't force you to see that. God knows I've tried, but I've failed. Only you can do that."

She backed away a few steps to lean against the wall and crossed her arms in front of her. "This isn't about me, Boyd. It's about the theft of Sam's lab notes. You're the only one who would have anything to gain from the loss of those notes, and you certainly had ample access to them, both at the laboratory and here in Sam's home."

"I notice you still call it Sam's home, not Paula's home."

"Don't try to divert my attention. It is Sam's home, just as much as it was when he still lived here. He bought this house, we raised a family here, and he died here."

"And you've turned it into a mausoleum where you can revere his memory and play the cloistered widow for the rest of your sterile life."

"*I am* widow. An unwise widow who trusted you."

"You want to blame me for the missing notes because you're afraid. Admit it, you don't want me to get close, and the best way to keep me at bay is to blame me for something so horrible you could never forgive me."

He held his hands at his sides and stepped toward her, stopping only inches from her, but he made no move to reach for her. "Am I so threatening, so near to fitting into your life that you can't give me credit for ethical behavior at least? You're right. I didn't want to get involved in this project, not because I didn't want to endorse Sam's work but because I didn't want us to get to know each other in these circumstances. I wanted to know you as Paula Wincott, someone with a new start, someone who would see me as I am, just a regular guy, not as her husband's mortal enemy."

She raised both hands to fend him off. "I can't get involved with you at all. You knew it from the beginning, and God forgive me, I knew it, too. You won me over the same way you won everyone else over. I allowed my emotions to blind me to everything."

He shook his head slightly and took a deep breath. "I don't win people over, Paula. I don't try to charm people, as you've accused. If I'm charming, it's because I like people, and my folks brought me up to treat others the way I would want to be treated." His lips lifted slightly in a wry grin. "The golden rule, I guess."

"You made love to me to further your own ends," she accused, voice breaking in despair.

He made no move to touch her but looked steadily into her eyes. "I made love to you because I love you."

She was stunned. Tremors ran through her body at his words. She had to lean against the wall to remain upright while her mind warred with her emotions. Closing her eyes against his declaration, she held him at bay with an accusation.

"You stole Sam's notes," she lashed at him, wishing with every heartbeat that it weren't true, wishing the problem could evaporate and they could start at the point where he said he loved her.

"Is that what you believe?"

She didn't answer. He stepped back, putting space between them. They faced each other without speaking. After a long moment, she hung her head. Still he waited.

At last, he turned up the collar of his jacket and opened the door. "I'm wasting my time here. I thought you knew me better than that. Believe whatever pleases you."

The door closed behind him, and the house felt too large for one small woman whose life was suddenly empty. She slowly slid down the wall to sit on the floor because her legs would no longer support her. Hot tears scalded rivulets down her cheeks.

She told herself she had done the right thing. But it didn't feel right. It hurt more than anything in her life had ever hurt.

More than Sam's death had hurt.

****

Boyd left with a mixture of righteous anger and a profound sense of defeat. Even his declaration of love had failed to move her. He couldn't take it back, nor did he want to. It was true. He loved her with every atom of his body and soul, passionately, completely, and forever. He sat in his car for an eternity, running a dozen scenarios in his mind, trying to find the key that he has missed in his efforts to free the woman he knew lived inside her.

But he was not willing to beat his head against the stone wall she had built around her heart. He had bloodied himself enough and deserved better treatment than what he'd received at her hands. For his own self respect he had to quit the field. And quit he would.

His first thought was to get blind, stinking drunk. But reason told him that tomorrow he would be no farther ahead, and that would leave him with one helluva hangover. On the drive to his house, he gathered his emotions together as much as he could and tried to plan the rest of his life without Paula.

The telephone rang as he walked through the door. The last thing he wanted to do was talk to anyone, but by force of habit he picked up the phone.

"Boyd, darling, I'm so glad I caught you. Guess who!"

He recognized the voice immediately. "I don't know. Who?"

A cascade of musical laughter followed. "Of course you know. It's Melissa."

The sound of her voice conjured a picture of honey-colored hair sweeping soft, creamy shoulders; amber eyes a man could fall into; long, supple legs that wrapped his waist to hold him deep inside. Beautiful Melissa who married Charlie Hampton.

He waited a beat. "Hello, Melissa. How's Charlie?"

She didn't seem to notice the lack of tone in his voice. But then, Melissa was always wrapped up in herself and her desires. "Oh, Boyd, I don't want to talk about him. We're divorced. He really wasn't everything I needed."

He tried to hold annoyance in check, but sarcasm rose to the surface. "You thought you needed him at the time. Or was it his money? A working professor couldn't give you all the luxuries you figured you deserved."

"Don't be mean, Boyd. I've thought about you over and over, wishing I'd married you instead of Charles."

"You had that option."

"Don't be so curt. You're not giving me a chance to explain."

"There's nothing to explain. Our relationship has been over for twelve years. I count myself lucky that you chose Charlie."

"I made a mistake. I was young and inexperienced."

His laugh was short, mirthless. "Thirty-three hardly counts as young and, as I recall, *very* experienced. I don't want to be rude, but why are you calling me? And how did you get my number?"

"Sheila didn't think you'd mind. Aren't you glad to hear from me? I've missed you so much."

His sister gave his number to a woman who hadn't crossed his mind in a decade? A woman who was the merry-go-round adventure of his life, who taught him what true love was not.

Melissa continued in her still-girlish voice that once held such sexual promise, "I've thought about us together so many times. I used to pretend it was you making love to me instead of Charles."

Boyd had heard enough. "Look, Melissa, I hope you're a happy divorcée. I hope you got a good settlement. But there's nothing for us to talk about. As tempting as a roll in the hay might be to contemplate, I'm very much in love with the only woman I'll ever want."

"I don't believe that. You left Montreal because I married Charles. It's your fault you and I couldn't be together," she whined. "We could have continued seeing each other. He didn't need to know."

The mere sound of her voice irritated him. "I'm hanging up now. Don't call me again."

"But Boyd, I've realized that I love you; I've always loved you."

He hung up the telephone, opened the refrigerator, and took out a beer. As he popped the tab and took a hearty swig, he reran his last remarks to Melissa. He was truly in love with the only woman he would ever want.

A woman he could never have.

CHAPTER TWENTY-ONE

A few days later, a telephone call from Lottie brought Paula long-awaited news. "I found the copies of the grant proposals you asked about. Shall I put them out for you?"

"Yes, please. I'll pick them up at—let's see, it's almost five o'clock. Are you going to be there for a while?"

"Sure thing. Come on down. I'll wait for you."

As promised, Lottie was waiting with a red folder on her desk. She didn't offer tea and didn't usher Paula into the lounge. She pulled up a chair next to her desk and patted it for Paula to sit.

"These are the copies I made of the grant proposals before I put them in the mail for Professor Mackenzie. I think this is what you were asking about." There was something indefinable in Lottie's tone, something Paula had never heard before, but she couldn't exactly put her finger on.

"Thanks very much. That's just what I was asking about."

"As you can see," Lottie continued, "a great deal of work went into these applications, long hours of work and lots of creative energy. It's not everyone has the knack for grant writing, you know. Professor Mackenzie is a crackerjack."

Paula thumbed through the forms. Lottie was correct. A mountain of work rested in her hands. She hadn't realized it was such a prodigious undertaking and mumbled something unintelligible.

"He took time away from his own lab," Lottie went on, "to meet with Sam's students so he could have the best and most recent test results to put into these papers. He wanted to make sure the proposals had every chance to win the most money, and he covered every base." She paused, then asked, "Why do you think he did that?"

Only half listening, Paula continued to absorb the magnitude of the effort Boyd had put into this project. "Yes, well, he accepted this assignment at Ed's insistence, you know. He didn't want to do it, what with the longtime feud between him and Sam. Ed didn't give him any choice. He bullied Boyd into doing it."

"Feud? The surprise in Lottie's tone irritated Paula. "What in the world are you talking about?"

"You don't have to pretend with me. I know how Boyd treated Sam, the jealousy and animosity, the repeated attempts to discredit him. Sam told me all about it. I'm sure it's what led to Sam's premature death. Boyd caused so much anxiety, Sam's heart couldn't take it."

Her tone was short, although she didn't mean it to be. She was simply so tired of the constant praise heaped on Boyd Mackenzie's head, the anger came through unbidden.

Lottie took off her glasses, then laid them on the table. Leaning close, she spoke slowly, with deliberate emphasis. "We all know about the jealousy and animosity, the repeated attempts to discredit Boyd, and the stress it caused in the department. Ed mediated any number of times when Sam made unfounded accusations against Boyd. But Boyd was largely unaware of Sam's dislike for him because Dr. King tried to handle it without fanfare. He likes to keep dissension out of his department."

Aghast, Paula said, "What are you talking about? You have it all backwards."

"You weren't here. All you have is Sam's paranoia. There was nothing on Boyd's part that would have caused any friction between them. Sam had been the star of the department for so many years, he just took it into his head that Boyd was trying to take the spotlight, and he couldn't tolerate it."

Paula would have stopped her, but Lottie seemed determined to have her say. "You must have seen how Sam changed over the last few years, how irritable he became. He was short tempered and sometimes completely irrational. That's why Dr. King had to ease him out of the classroom, which he blamed on Boyd, of course. Fortunately, he never turned his anger toward Dr. King.

"He began to make mistakes in the lab, so he was encouraged to let his graduate students take over the actual work of experimentation and notating the results."

Paula couldn't assimilate the information. She didn't want to believe what Lottie was saying, but Lottie had no reason to lie. She had been one of Sam's biggest fans for twenty years.

"Please, stop. I can't hear this. It's not true." Burying her face in her hands, she sobbed, "I won't let it be true."

But Lottie, fair-minded and ineffably honest, continued. "But, it *is* true. I know it's not what you want to believe, certainly not what Sam wanted you to believe, not even what he believed. We all allowed you to live in ignorance these years because we didn't see any harm. But now it's time for you to recognize that our Sam had deteriorated and tried to damage the reputation of a fine man. Not because Sam was a bad person but because of circumstances he couldn't control."

It felt like the world had tumbled around her ears. Sam senile? It wasn't possible. He wasn't that old. And he was her perfect Sam, perfect in every way. "I can't listen to any more. And I can't sit here if you're going to go on like that." She stood up to make ready to go.

Lottie nodded. "I understand. You've been bombarded with information overload. But sit down. I have more news that I know you'll find of interest."

Paula sat gingerly, ready to spring up at the first sign of unwelcome information. Lottie pulled a sheaf of papers from the top drawer of her desk, laid them on the desk, and put her reading glasses back on. She scanned the top sheet, then took off the glasses and looked steadily at Paula.

"You wanted to know where the money came from that bought the new equipment and paid the students' back pay. It's all here, if you want to read it. Boyd Mackenzie diverted funds from his own biochemistry lab to make sure Sam's lab got what it needed. That's why he was so cagey when you asked him about it. He didn't tell Ed or me about it. I know only because I went digging." Smiling enigmatically, she shoved the papers toward Paula. "You'd be surprised at the connections a secretary has."

Paula looked at the papers but didn't see them. Her vision was blurred by the intensity of the emotions racing through her. Nothing made sense, everything was a lie, her life was not real.

"Here's the clincher," Lottie said. "He borrowed money with his house as collateral. If those grants don't come through, he'll have to find the money to pay back the loan."

"But why? Why would he do something like that?"

Lottie folded her hands on the desk. "Why indeed? Do you mean to say you don't know the answer to that question? Or should I say the answers to that question. Because there are more reasons than just one. Surely you have some idea. You can't be that unaware."

"No," Paula whispered, unwilling to consider

Lottie's point. "I don't know the answer."

"Then I guess you'll have to ask him yourself."

Paula's head snapped up angrily. "I can't. I won't. He's the one that stole Sam's laboratory notes and no doubt destroyed them so that we can never replicate his work. He's been pretending to help, but all the while he was exactly what Sam said he was. You've all been conned by his good looks and superficial charm."

Helpless, she flailed her arms. "I include myself in that group. He had me fooled as well, and I made it easy for him to get into the lab. I sent him to talk to Barry Connors. I even let him into my house and into Sam's personal effects. How could I have been so stupid?"

Lottie sat very still until Paula's tidal wave of pain ebbed. Her face betrayed no emotion, and when she spoke at last, her voice was soothing. "If that's what you think, then you have quite a lot on your plate. Quite a lot. You have some thinking to do so I'd best let you go so you can start working it out."

She handed Paula a tissue and stood, signaling the conversation was over. Reeling inwardly, Paula buttoned her coat and made a swift exit. She needed fresh air and time to think.

****

Paula was emotionally drained when she arrived home. Why did Lottie say all of those terrible things about Sam? Everyone knew and loved him. Paula had built her whole life around him, knowing him, trusting him, admiring him. Now Lottie wanted to destroy a whole life. Why?

It no longer mattered. She wouldn't have to see Boyd Mackenzie again. She would sign up with Professor Sloan for 202 in the next term. She would continue with a dramatic literature course, perhaps take the art course Emma had suggested. That would take up her time very nicely and would allow her a creative outlet as well. She would rearrange her life again.

This time it would fit the normal parameters that had circumscribed her life before Boyd Mackenzie came into it.

Her relationship with him had been an aberration, and she needed to restore equanimity. After all, as Emma had suggested, she was too old for such unseemly behavior. Romance and sexual passion certainly had their place, but not in an over-the-hill grandmother. And certainly not with the man who had destroyed her husband's professional life.

She would have to accept that Sam's lab would be turned over to the new researcher in the fall. If the new professor was interested in conductivity, perhaps Sam's early experiments would be salvaged. Or perhaps the research would take a new direction. In any event, it would no longer be Sam's lab. Another chapter in her life was closed, and she would have to make the best of what was left.

One of Lottie's statements replayed over and over again in her head. Boyd had borrowed money against his house in order to pay the salaries for Sam's lab assistants. He could have paid the money back when the grants came in, of course. But, if the notes were stolen, the work couldn't continue, and there would be no grant money. He could lose his house.

Why would he have put himself in such a vulnerable position?

CHAPTER TWENTY-TWO

Professor Sloan was a kindly, albeit somewhat plodding, chemistry teacher with excellent student rapport. Paula felt an immediate kinship with him. She asked cogent questions in class and participated fully, as she would have been unable to do if she had stayed in Boyd's 201 class last fall. The other students treated her as a peer, and she found she was enjoying chemistry again as she had when she had taken her first class with Sam so many years ago.

Her dramatic literature course was a joy because of the continued enthusiasm of Professor Corrigan, who gave extra credit for attending theater productions in Boulder and Denver. He arranged group excursions to local productions, and Paula was always eager to participate. Not only did she enjoy the plays, but the class discussions following the production were always lively and interesting. Almost all of the assigned reading touched on social issues as well as interpersonal relationships, and she was often surprised to find there was a wide gap between her point of view and the attitudes of the very young students.

She began to realize that Emma was right— times had changed while she wasn't looking. She was getting an education in more ways than one. Young women were a lot more liberated than when she was their age. The sexual revolution had happened while she was making a home for husband and family, and she had somehow missed knowing about it.

Weeks went by, and she filled them with anything that would take her mind off Boyd, but she found herself looking for him when she met her Biochemistry 201 class. Did she fear she might see him, or was she hoping? She didn't know anymore. He was no longer a part of her life, but something in her wanted to catch a glimpse of him, even if just for a fleeting moment.

In those first few weeks, she had worried that he would continue to pursue her or at least would continue to try to clear himself of any blame. She was surprised that he didn't. In fact, he made no attempt to see her, not even a telephone call. Well, that was what she wanted, no contact with him at all. She could never forgive him, nor could she forget his words of love.

In the bosom of her family she found strong support for her position, and she sought it often. No one knew of her true relationship with him, and for that she was profoundly grateful. At least she hadn't made a fool of herself in front of those whose opinion mattered so much. But still there was that little flutter in her heart when she thought about him. No one had stirred her like Boyd—not even Sam, she finally admitted. And that admission staggered her.

Lottie had asked Paula to be matron of honor at her wedding, and Paula had eagerly accepted. Lottie had no close women friends, but Paula had shared so many years of tea and sympathy with her that they had become close. And wedding plans had the knack of pulling women together from time immemorial. Ah, the bonding power of weddings and baby showers.

Lottie had been nervous when she and Paula made their first visit to the bridal shop, but the friendly sales woman put her at ease immediately. "Is this a first or second marriage?" she asked. "We have a wide range of services for either, and I can assure you we offer whatever style suits your needs."

As Lottie was embarrassed to admit it was her first wedding, Paula jumped in. "It's a first and only, so we want it to be memorable."

The saleslady nodded. "Of course. I'm glad to see you've brought your friend. This is a very delicate time in a woman's life. We have found a friend often helps stabilize the impact of all the planning that's needed. Please take a seat. I'll bring over our book and samples."

They sat on a mauve velvet love seat while awaiting the saleslady. "Jamie and I made up a budget for the wedding and reception, but I'll need your help to keep from running right over the top," Lottie whispered. "Everything is so beautiful, it'll be hard not to overspend, but I want everything to be right, you know?"

"I hadn't thought about the financial aspect of it," admitted Paula. "When Sam and I got married, my family paid for everything. I never even considered the expense."

"What about when Emma married Wesley?"

"We had an amazing wedding planner. Sam gave her a budget. Emma told her what she and Wesley wanted, and she took care of all the details."

"But it's such fun to do the planning, don't you think?" Lottie asked.

"You're right; I think it is," Paula said, getting into the excitement of it all. "We'll work together to keep you within your budget."

Paula had never had a budget. Sam had taken care of the finances, paid the bills, bought the house, the car, and such. She had charge accounts at all of the major stores, so she just bought what she needed, and the bills were paid. Since Sam's death, she had allowed Wesley to handle her accounts until recently when he insisted she had to learn to take care of herself. She didn't like it at first, but she had gradually come to find it freeing.

"I want a wedding dress that I can use for fancy affairs after we're married," Lottie explained. "There's no point wearing something one time only to put it away in tissue forever. Each time I wear the dress it will remind me of our wedding and how much I love my Jamie."

Lottie's face glowed with a rush of emotion that touched Paula's heart. She thought of her own wedding dress, wrapped in tissue and boxed in the attic. She hadn't taken it out since their wedding. Poor dress. It had cost thousands of dollars, and she had worn it for only a matter of hours before relegating it to storage.

"You're absolutely right. Let's find something very special that you can wear for the rest of your marriage, your *dress of love.*"

They giggled like schoolgirls, then hugged. After examining what seemed like a hundred beautiful dresses, they found a gorgeous ivory silk with silver lace inserts that matched Lottie's now-highlighted silver hair. Tiny pearls outlined the lace and drew the eye upward to the wearer's face. The cut was generous and complimentary to Lottie's full figure, and, with the hem at knee length, it could be worn for any and all dress-up occasions. It was perfect. A wide-brimmed, gauzy tulle hat completed the picture.

Lottie ordered a bouquet of yellow roses and baby's breath and a white carnation boutonnière for Jamie. Paula was to wear pale pink, so Lottie picked a bridesmaid's bouquet of pink rosebuds wrapped in white satin ribbons.

"With your hair and coloring, you'll be a vision in pink," Lottie assured her. "Like cotton candy."

"It doesn't matter so much how I'll look. What's important is that you'll be a beautiful bride."

"It is my day, and I want everything to be a

vision of loveliness. And you're a part of it."

Paula was humbled by Lottie's selflessness and felt a swell of emotion threaten to spill onto her cheeks. She was impressed with Lottie's ability to make decisions and handle every aspect of her wedding with authority and aplomb. This in no way diminished Lottie's femininity or charm, as Sam had always insisted it did. Quite the contrary, she seemed to blossom with the richness of the task she had undertaken.

After they had looked through a book of about a hundred cakes, they agreed on a simple yet elegant three-tiered confection that fit within the financial parameters Lottie and Jamie had set. They left the shop in high spirits and made their way to a little coffee house on Pearl Street where they ordered a strong Colombian brew and sinful delicacies from the pastry cart.

The spring sun was shining through the glass window, and they were in a little bubble of suspended time. Paula was suddenly struck with the realization that this particular moment would never come again. It was a unique gift to be savored while it existed, then consigned to golden memory.

"Are you happy?" she asked, knowing the answer already.

Lottie's face gave her away. "I never knew I could be so happy," she said with a sigh. "The young people don't know what they're missing, and that's a fact. I was so much in love with young Terry when I was a girl. We were going to be married and live a long, happy life together. But I didn't have as much to offer him as I now have to offer James. I was only a slip of a thing, not knowing much about the world, the true relationship of marriage and love."

She leaned slightly forward and winked. "That old song is right, you know. Love is better the second time around."

Paula felt a stab in her midsection. Boyd was different from Sam in so many ways. Lovemaking with him was certainly richer and more creative than with Sam, but was it better? And lovemaking was not the same as love.

She caught Lottie's hand and asked in earnest, "How is it better? And how do you know it's love and not just lustful infatuation? You've been alone for a long time, so how can you trust your judgment?"

Lottie returned Paula's squeeze before releasing it to pick up her fork. "Oh, honey, it's not hard at all. There's physical attraction, of course. Just like the first time. Great sex is still great sex." Her cheeks reddened in a modest blush. "But there's other things that are important as you get older. There are so many things to share, so you want someone you like as a person, someone you can trust, someone who really cares about you as a person, who encourages your own personal growth, even at the risk of your growing away from him."

She smiled, then picked up another piece of pastry. "James has encouraged me to explore my own interests, whether he shares them or not. For example, I've always wanted to learn French, but he has no interest in a second language, so he signed me up for French lessons. He says when we visit France he'll rely on his wife to do all the talking."

Paula was surprised. "You're going to France?"

"We haven't made firm plans, but we're talking about a vacation next year. He's not particularly keen on France, but he knows it's a dream of mine, so he's taking me—after I learn a little of the language, of course."

"That sounds like such fun. Sam made a lot of trips to France, but it was always for conferences or book tours. He said I would have been bored, so we agreed I would stay home with the children." Paula moved her fork aimlessly around the plate. "I wish I could have gone with him just once. Maybe I wouldn't have been bored."

"It's not too late," Lottie declared. "Why don't you go there on your own? You're a single woman with time and money to do anything you want. Or go to Italy. Or England, if you don't speak any foreign language."

Her initial response was to decline. "What would the kids say? I just hear Emma pooh-poohing the idea. What would they think about me gallivanting off to Europe?"

Lottie was aghast. "Girl, why would you care what Emma thinks? She's your daughter, not the arbiter of modern behavior. I can't believe you would even consider her opinion for a millisecond before making a decision, though I hope she would encourage you to explore the world and enjoy the things that please you. If she doesn't, then she's not on your team."

Though Lottie's point of view surprised and confused her, Paula mulled over the prospect as they finished up their coffee and Lottie took her leave.

When she got home, Paula picked up the telephone to call Emma, but at the last moment she put the receiver back in its cradle. Maybe she wouldn't ask Emma's opinion after all.

CHAPTER TWENTY-THREE

Paula no longer stopped at the Chemistry office when she was on campus. It was too depressing to know that Sam's lab had been closed pending the arrival of the new faculty member. Plus, she wanted to avoid contact with Boyd. From time to time she passed him as she walked either to or from her chemistry class. He always nodded, face betraying nothing more than polite acknowledgement. She was equally polite but distant. It was as if they had never known each other in anything but a formal setting.

She no longer fumed when she thought of his theft. Instead, she had a bruised spot on her heart that grew larger as time went on. She wished he had confessed his crime so she could have closure, but she knew that would never happen.

She had thought carefully about what Lottie had told her about the diversion of Boyd's funding to Sam's lab and had tried to reconcile it to the behavior of a man intent on destroying a colleague. She had seen the evidence that he had indeed written an excellent grant proposal and it had been submitted promptly. What did Boyd have to gain personally from such apparently selfless acts? Ultimately she concluded that, by doing so, he had gained her trust as well as access to Sam's laboratory. Time and money well spent if it gave him the opportunity to destroy Sam's work.

But what about the loan? How would he pay it back? That tape kept playing in her head, but she couldn't find the answer.

The weeks rolled by so swiftly it appeared that

spring would break any day. Boulder weather could be unpredictable, but usually mid-March saw an end to the snowfalls and the abrupt appearance of daffodils, crocuses, violets, and tulips. This year Spring was peeking around the corner, making promises to show up early.

Boyd continued teaching his section of Chemistry 202, noting Paula's absence each time the class met. He knew she had registered for another section, and he had to rely on chance meetings just to get a glimpse of her, even though he knew that was all he would ever have of her. He frequently stopped in at the office, hoping she might be having tea with Lottie, but she was obviously avoiding him. The last time he had made an excuse to stop by, Lottie had given him an appraising eye. "Good morning, Professor. I'm afraid she's not here, but I'm happy to see you."

Was he that obvious?

"Lottie, my darlin', you know I came by most particularly to see you. And how is the blushing bride-to-be on this glorious spring morning?" He was overdoing it, but couldn't seem to find the middle road.

"Now don't play the innocent with me, she chided. You've been mooning over Paula for six months, and believe me it's no secret. Come and have a sit-down with me. I think you need a cup of tea and a very large piece of coffee cake."

She was already moving to the buffet that held mugs, gesturing to a comfy seat in the lounge. Seeing no reason to refuse, he laid down his briefcase and settled his rangy frame into a soft leather chair.

Lottie chatted while she poured tea and cut fresh cake. "Why didn't you tell her you didn't steal Sam's papers?"

"You really cut to the chase."

She tossed him a cryptic look over one shoulder. "Life is too short, Professor. We can't wait around for advantages to come to us. We have to make our own luck. I've learned that very recently, and it's now my core philosophy. You must forgive me if I proselytize."

She placed a steaming mug of tea before him and set the plate of coffee cake in the center of the side table before she took a seat on the sofa across from him. "Why didn't you tell her?"

Boyd rubbed a tired hand across his chin. "I told her repeatedly there was no bad blood between Sam and me, at least not on my part. She has some wild notion that we were mortal enemies. No matter what I said or did, I couldn't convince her otherwise. I thought I was making progress, then all of a sudden she accused me of stealing Sam's experiments."

"And you never told her the thief was Amy Hastings and that she destroyed the lab notes?"

He picked up the mug, let it warm his hands. "I didn't."

"Why not? She's not likely to hear it from anyone else since you kept the whole thing so hush-hush."

"I didn't want to embarrass Amy's family. She's not entirely stable, and I thought it best to handle it quietly and let it pass. It won't bring the notes back, and it isn't fair to Amy. That's why I asked that it be kept within the department."

"Then didn't you clear yourself with Paula?"

He thought for a moment before he answered. "Because I'm tired of defending myself against unjust accusations. I'm ready for someone to know me and trust me. She immediately jumped to the conclusion that she had been right about me all along, that I had underhandedly conned her to get to those notes to destroy Sam's reputation."

He shifted in his seat and leaned forward. "I'm a nice guy, an honest man, and I deserve better than that."

"Yes," she agreed. "My mother always told me people will treat you they way you let them treat you. And I've found that to be true my whole life. But I hate to see the two of you lose each other because you're both so bull-headed. I'll explain it to her myself."

He was quick to respond. "No. If you bail me out this time, who'll bail me out the next time she takes some crackpot thought into her head? I don't want to waste my time explaining and justifying. If she loves me, she has to trust me. I've done everything I can to build a relationship of honesty and reliability, and she refuses to believe any of it. I won't let you run interference for me."

"All right. But I hope she comes to her senses before it's too late. There's many a woman out there who would count herself lucky to snag you." She added with a wink, "Why, if I weren't so gone on my James, I'd let you keep your old promises to me."

He gave her a wry chuckle. "If you weren't so gone on your James, I'd have to challenge him to a fight for taking you away. But, since you're obviously taken with him, I don't want to give him any unnecessary grief." He rose to collect his briefcase. "Thanks for letting me bend your ear. Sorry to be such a whiner."

"Any time, Professor. My ear is yours."

Outside the door, Boyd stopped to zip up his bomber jacket and caught sight of Paula as she came out of class. She was chatting with another student as they walked along the hallway, and she failed to notice Boyd until she was almost upon him. She said good-bye to the girl and turned to exit the building. Suddenly she looked up, caught sight of him, and missed a step. Her books slipped from her fingers, slid across the floor, and landed very nearly at his feet.

Frozen in place, his heart pounded like a trip hammer. As she made no move to retrieve her books, he knelt to recover them and return them to her arms. As he handed them back to her, their fingers touched, and he found himself tightening his grip on her hands. He looked into her face. She was flushed as pink as the fuzzy sweater she wore under her coat. He wanted to slide his arms under that coat and pull her close to him. He wanted to feel her breasts against his chest, even if only for a moment. His body went hard at the thought.

"Paula." He whispered her name so softly he wasn't sure she heard him. He wasn't even sure he had said it aloud or whether her name was simply running through his head.

With an effort, he dropped her hands and stepped back to allow her to pass.

****

Outside, Paula clutched her books close to her chest and stumbled past him, her body shaking with tremors she couldn't control. His effect on her was still electric, and she had to fight to keep from throwing herself into his arms. The sexual pull was elemental and raw, something that loomed between them like a palpable force that neither could harness. It almost had tangible form, and that that frightened her more than anything.

She shook her head to clear it and hurried to her Dramatic Literature class across campus. She found her usual seat and opened her book to the current assignment, Ibsen's *Ghosts*.

She had found it a fascinating play about the sins of the fathers visited upon the children. The long-suffering wife should have left her philandering husband years ago, but because of society's rigid rules, she had not. As a result, she had contracted venereal disease from her husband and had passed it along to their son.

The classroom discussion turned lively, and she participated fully, as usual. She had lost her fear of looking foolish in the eyes of the other students. She had come to realize that their opinions had no more intrinsic value than her own, and, in fact, the class seemed to value her thoughts, coming as they did from a different generation with different interpretations. Sometimes she even incited spirited debate, and she left the class feeling endorsed. Maybe, just maybe, Emma would be proud of her.

The next assigned reading was Ibsen's *A Doll's House*. It had been a groundbreaking play that had shocked society when it was first performed. She was eager to read it and make notes for the next class discussion.

That night, after dinner, she poured herself a glass of sweet dessert wine and settled down to read. As she began the play, it seemed like the usual conventional setting. Nora was married to Torvald, who appeared to adore her. They had two small children with whom Nora enjoyed a warm, playful relationship. Torvald, an older man, clearly catered to his young Nora and took care that she had no worries or concerns other than being his wife and the mother of his children.

Paula felt warmed by the comparison of this relationship with hers and Sam's. Torvald handled the finances, and Nora knew nothing of his business affairs. She was an innocent, and he loved her innocence. In one telling scene, he asked Nora to dance for him, which she did playfully, and he responded by catching her in his arms and making love to her.

Paula wondered, in passing, why the play was entitled *A Doll's House* but let the thought go as she was enjoying the story so much. By the end of the play, she had gained massive food for thought.

As it progressed, it became clear that Torvald insisted on Nora's remaining a child in the doll's house he provided for her. He did not want a partner, an equal, a wife. The one time she had acted the part of an adult wife and saved him from financial ruin, he berated her, upbraided her, and threatened her with his towering rage.

Ultimately, Nora had to leave Torvald in order to grow into a mature woman. He had inhibited her personal growth and kept her a perpetual child. It took an emotional upheaval to bring their conflict to the surface.

Cole's Notes gave a thorough critique of the play, explaining the social mores of the time when the play was written. The rules were such that a wife did not leave her husband, so Nora's departure at the end of the play was incomprehensible to contemporary audiences.

Ibsen was an early feminist, however, so his point was keenly made: women are not children, not toys, not playthings to be enjoyed and then put away in a drawer, only to be taken out at the owner's pleasure.

Paula couldn't help but see the parallel in her own life. It was as if she had worn a blindfold all of her life and now it had been removed. The light of awareness was too bright. She wasn't sure what she saw, but it was a different world. All the love Sam had shown her had been tempered by his sense of ownership. Any time she evinced an interest in anything outside the home, he would call her attention to her responsibilities to the children and the home, using guilt as a tool to keep her domesticated.

But he had been right, hadn't he? She did have responsibilities, and she really didn't have time for activities outside the home. He had to be right. He was Sam Wincott. He knew how life was supposed to go.

She remembered how Helen King used to call her to have lunch or take in a movie or go shopping during the day. She always declined because Sam didn't like for her to be away from the house. He felt she should be available in case the children needed anything, even when they were in school. And it seemed inappropriate to him that she should have her own friends. After all, they were a married couple, weren't they?

Eventually, Helen stopped issuing invitations, and Paula had been relieved because she didn't have to experience Sam's lectures on correct behavior. Life was simple and uncluttered.

Even their love life was at his direction. He decided when and how they would make love. As a young girl, she thought it romantic that he made the approach, but as she grew older, she felt confident enough to make the first move sometimes. He had explained to her that it was the male role to initiate sex and that it was unbecoming and indelicate for a woman to do so. He initiated it often, and his lovemaking was expert and completely satisfying, but she always accommodated his schedule, not the other way around.

She, like Nora, had been kept in a state of arrested development. It was mind numbing to consider all of the ramifications. In need of another perspective, she phoned Helen King and made arrangements to meet her for lunch.

CHAPTER TWENTY-FOUR

Paula arrived at the little coffee shop early. The area was busy, as usual. Boulder city fathers had wisely limited growth, and it had remained clearly a college town—clean, upscale, and hospitable.

Fresh-faced girls in Birkenstocks sold organic muffins, and more than one shop supplied botanical lotions and beauty supplies. The bars sold only 3.2 beer to students, and rowdiness was kept to a minimum. The Hill reflected those aspects, and the coffee shop was a mecca for delicious, wholesome, and well-prepared food served by friendly staff.

She stepped inside to find Helen already seated at a table by the window. After a quick hello and hug, they settled themselves with menus.

While Paula studied hers, Helen chatted happily. "I'm so glad we finally got to have a girl lunch. I've so much wanted us to be friends all of these years, you know."

The waitress arrived to take their order, served them iced tea in tall frosted glasses with thick slices of lemon perched on the rim, and left them to visit.

Paula tried to sidle into the conversation, hoping she wouldn't be too obvious. "I'm sorry it took so long for us to get together. You know how it was when Sam was alive."

She hoped that would give Helen an opening to enlarge on the topic, but Helen was cagey. "Well, I know you were always very busy with this and that. But I'm glad you have some time now. Of course, I always enjoyed the times when the four of us got together, but you and I never had the chance to spend time together, just us girls. So I never had a strong sense of your personality or your opinions. You know, one on one."

She squeezed a large slice of lemon into her glass and reached for the sugar bowl. "As I recall, Sam always had such strong opinions and no hesitation in expressing them, so I just assumed he spoke for both of you."

So people thought she didn't have an opinion. Paula twiddled with her iced tea spoon and kept her eyes downcast. "I guess he did speak for both of us. Not because I didn't have a point of view, but because he was older, more knowledgeable, more experienced. I thought he was always right. So if my opinion differed from his, I thought I was wrong and had best not offer one." She didn't add that he had explained that very fact to her on more than one occasion.

Helen visibly flinched. "Really?"

"I know it sounds silly when I say it out loud, but I always felt inadequate around Sam. He was just about perfect, and I felt so lucky to be married to him."

Looking baffled, Helen said, "He was a fine man, but he was also lucky to be married to you. You have so much to offer, and you'll forgive me for saying it, but I don't think Sam every really appreciated all of your wonderful qualities. I don't mean to speak ill of the dead, but you've blossomed in this last year, and I don't think that would have been possible while you were married to him."

There. It was out in the open. She could talk about it now.

"Tell me," she began tentatively. "Did my marriage appear different from other faculty marriages? I mean, did it seem to anyone, you especially, that our relationship was in any way unusual?"

She didn't know how to tackle the question, but she hoped Helen would pick up on what she was asking. If Helen understood, she was too wary to answer without more information.

"Different in what way?"

Okay, Paula knew she would have to work a little harder. "I always thought we had a storybook marriage. You know, I was eighteen when we got married, and I thought the universe revolved around Sam. Whatever he said I took as gospel because I was young and inexperienced. He never encouraged me to develop my own character, my own personality or my own point of view. I thought that was fine because he had all of those things in abundance. Enough for both of us, I guess," she finished weakly.

The new Paula realized how foolish her explanation sounded.

"I see," Helen replied noncommittally.

"Do you?" Paula twisted her napkin, trying to work up enough courage to ask the question that was on her mind. "Since he's been gone, I'm seeing the world differently, and it's been very confusing."

"In what way?"

"People treat me like Paula, not like Sam's wife. They ask me questions, and they expect answers. Answers I don't necessarily have."

"That's bad?"

"I don't know. I'm... I'm not explaining this very well, am I?" She paused for a moment before plunging forward. "Have you read *A Doll's House*, the play by Henrik Ibsen?"

Helen nodded appreciatively. "Why, yes. We read it in my sophomore year at Berkley. And about ten years ago, it was produced here at the university theater. Ed and I saw it with Professor Sloan and his wife. Excellent production. I remember the student who played Torvald was very impressive for such a youngster. Why do you ask?"

Paula enunciated each word painfully. "I think I've been living in a doll's house for thirty-two years."

Helen looked at Paula with a dawning comprehension. "You mean you didn't know it all this time?"

Paula's neck began to prickle. "You mean you did?"

"My dear, it was obvious Sam was the kind of man who controlled everything in his sphere of influence. You were the dutiful young wife who ran his household and raised his children. Why do you think he chose someone so much younger?"

"I thought we were like everyone else."

"I tried so many times to give you a glimpse of life on the outside, but I couldn't even get you to have a cup of coffee with me. Do you realize this is the first lunch we've ever had together in all the years we've known each other?"

The waitress placed their plates in front of them, and Helen tucked into her chicken, but Paula had lost her appetite. She was embarrassed. No, she was mortified.

"Why didn't you say anything?"

Helen broke off a piece of French baguette and slathered it with soft butter before answering. "Because it wasn't anyone's business except yours and Sam's. Whatever you had between you was what worked for you. Just as my relationship with Ed works for me. You were obviously successful for thirty-two years. Who am I to tamper with that?"

Paula watched Helen cut her chicken and spear a piece of tomato, but was unable to eat. Her stomach turned somersaults over an impending sense of dread. She didn't want to ask, but she had to know. "Helen, there's something I have to ask and I don't want you to sugarcoat the answer. Please, it's very important."

"Yes," Helen answered between bites.

"Did Ed share his work with you? I mean, what goes on with the faculty and things like that?"

"Of course. I've always been his sounding board. Why do you ask?"

"Are you aware of his relationship with Boyd Mackenzie?"

Helen took a long sip of iced tea, then clasped her hands on the table. "All right. But remember, you asked."

Paula nodded. And held her breath.

"Boyd came on high recommendation from a number of reliable sources. The entire department, including Sam, was enthusiastic when Ed decided to hire him. He seemed to fit right in. He made friends with the other faculty, and he really got the biochemistry area moving forward. He and Sam were friendly and appeared to get along. They were both charmers from the get-go, so they were popular with faculty and students."

"Helen, I need to know what happened," she urged, still not entirely sure she wanted to hear the truth.

Helen took a long breath. "Little by little, Sam began to take a dislike to Boyd. Small things in the beginning. Sam made critical remarks at first. If anyone disagreed, he would become angry. As time went on, he avoided Boyd completely, except for staff meetings or faculty functions. You know, those dinners and dances you never attended."

"Yes," Paula said. "Sam always said I would be bored. He said the other faculty spouses were educated and that I wouldn't understand their conversation."

"Interesting," Helen mused, opening another pat of butter for a fresh crust of bread. "We always wondered why you weren't there. All the other wives came, and we would have loved to have you join us.

Anyway, it just got worse as time went on, and finally Sam began to rant against Boyd, making unfounded accusations. He created such a poisonous environment that Ed was finally forced to remove Sam from the classroom."

She chewed a mouthful of endive salad and washed it down with a sip of tea. "You remember that. It was very unpleasant."

"Yes," Paula granted.

She remembered the rage Sam was in when he arrived home and how he railed against Boyd as the source of his frustration. His tirade went on for days, and she had been unable to console him. He considered Ed blameless, centering his venom solely on Boyd.

"Boyd has been largely unaware of the discord because Ed has tried to handle the matter discreetly," Helen said. "Ed didn't argue with Sam. It wouldn't have done any good, and it would have caused a rift between longtime friends. So he just moved the pieces around as best he could. He used to talk to me at length about how to keep the peace."

Inch by inch, Paula felt the floor drop from beneath her feet. Everything Boyd had said was true. Lottie confirmed it—only Paula hadn't believed her.

Helen laid it out clearly and caught Paula's eye. "Boyd Mackenzie is a good man. You could do a lot worse."

"My God, does everyone know?"

"Pretty much." Helen grinned saucily. "Certainly everyone who's seen his face whenever he's around you. A person would have to be blind not to see it." She finished up her chicken and wiped her mouth. "Ed and I talked about nothing else the night of the dance when you and Boyd were together on the floor. The heat in the room went up by fifty degrees when you two saw each other. I found it quite charming."

Paula leaned her elbow on the table and covered her eyes with her hand. "I feel as if my entire life is unraveling right before my eyes."

"We asked you up to the cabin because we knew Boyd was going to be at his cabin for the week, and we were trying our hand at matchmaking. We were going to manufacture an opportunity for you two to spend some time together, but it didn't work out. We were disappointed."

Paula kept silent, trying to work through the major amounts of information.

"I think you two are perfect for each other. Obviously, he thinks so, too." Helen signaled the waitress for the dessert tray. "You know he'll be at Lottie's wedding. You can't avoid him forever. And why would you? He's a gorgeous hunk of studliness, and he wants you. Lucky girl."

Paula laid her napkin on the table. "Would you excuse me? I need time alone to sort through all the information you've given me. I don't mean to run out on you, but I'm sure you understand. My head is stuffed."

At that exact moment, the arrival of the dessert tray captured Helen's attention. "Of course, my dear. I hope we can do this again some time. Lunch, I mean."

Paula virtually dashed out the door, pausing only long enough to toss over her shoulder, "Give my regards to Ed.

But Helen was engrossed in a choice between pecan pie and lemon tart.

The moment Paula arrived home, she sat down and wrote a long-overdue e-mail to Morgan, hoping he would pick it up wherever he was. With the miracle of fully-functioning laptops, he was able to communicate from whatever city he happened to be visiting, and did so with some regularity as his work took him all over the world.

With sweaty fingers, she typed a long note to him, hoping to gain support for the direction her life was taking. She knew she would not get that support from Emma, but she was hoping Morgan's point of view would be different, as it had always been.

Morgan had always opposed his father's autocratic manner, and they had butted heads from the time Morgan was a little boy. He had deliberately chosen to avoid any relationship with Sam's interests, and his move to Europe was largely to become his own man, separate from Sam. He did not, as Emma did, worship at Sam's feet, nor did he accept his father's opinion without due consideration. He had been an independent thinker from his youth, and Paula had refereed many a battle until Morgan moved away.

The next morning, she was relieved to find his answer blinking from her computer monitor. Strong, reliable Morgan had come through for her.

"Dear Mom,

So, you've finally started thinking for yourself, eh? Congratulations and welcome to the real world. Sorry if I sound a little sarcastic; I don't mean it that way. It's just that you were under Dad's thumb for so long, I thought he might have stunted your growth permanently. I'm astounded to hear your good news. I won't lecture. Suffice it to say you've come a long way, and I believe you've done yourself more of a favor than you know. It'll come to you as years go by, piece by piece.

I won't badmouth him because he was my father, and I loved him, but you have your own life now, and you are capable of making your own decisions. Emma will come around. She may be shortsighted, but she's not a mean-spirited person. And she loves you.

You know I thought your plan to go back to

school was an excellent one, and I'm proud of you for doing it."

Tears blurred Paula's vision as she absorbed the words she so needed to hear.

"I would love to see a new man in your life, Mom, and if you've found one that treats you right, I applaud you and welcome him. If it turns out that you and this unnamed fellow find romance and companionship, you must then tell me more about him. Keep your secret for now, if you want, but I'm keen to hear all about him when you're ready.

Morgan"

Bless her stable, reliable, wise son. She felt stronger just having him in her corner.

She picked up the telephone and dialed Emma's number. The answering machine picked up, and Emma's voice advised the caller to leave a message. Paula was well prepared.

"Hello, darling. I'm sorry I missed you. I had hoped we could talk. But we can do that later. Ask Wesley to call off any investigation about your dad's missing papers. Boyd Mackenzie didn't take them. I don't care to discuss it. Just stop any questioning of anyone."

As she went on, Paula found herself talking easily and with confidence. *"In answer to your question about the man who made love with me. It is a man whom I love and who says he loves me. If he's willing, he's the man I hope to marry. That man is Boyd Mackenzie, and I hope you'll come to respect him and trust him as I do."*

CHAPTER TWENTY-FIVE

In the last few days, Paula felt as if she had grown taller and had become more powerful. It was a physical sensation like one she had never experienced. It gave her the impetus to make the inevitable move that only she could make.

She skipped class the next day and went instead to Boyd's office during his regular office hours. With her heart thudding, she rapped on his door. No answer. She double checked the office hours. He should be in. She knocked a little harder, but there was no response. She tore a scrap of paper from her notebook and scribbled a quick note—"*Call me.*"

After sliding it beneath his door, she made her way to the chemistry office. She stuck her head in the door. "Lottie, is Professor Mackenzie in today?"

Lottie called from behind a file cabinet, "Oh, hi, Paula. No, dear, he said he's taking a few days off. I think he's going away, maybe up to the cabin. I'm not sure."

She didn't want to share her personal life with Lottie, but she needed information. "Does he have a telephone up there?"

"I don't think so. I think he goes up there to get away from telephones. I don't think he even takes his cell."

"Do you know how long he plans to be gone?"

Lottie closed the file drawer and brought an armful of files to her desk. She placed them in the OUT box on her desk before she answered. "No, I really don't. I'm sorry." She assessed Paula carefully. "Is there anything I can do for you?"

Paula's shoulders drooped perceptively. She shook her head and turned toward the door. "Thanks. There's nothing anyone can do."

She drove around for hours, aimlessly, thinking about everything she had said and done, how unfair she had been, how wrong she had been. She became increasingly depressed as she considered her own shortcomings. Then she decided. She would bare her soul to the Kings and ask for directions to Boyd's cabin at Estes Park. She would drive to wherever he was. It didn't matter. She had to see him.

She was grateful that Helen asked no questions and made no comment other than to give explicit directions to Boyd's cabin. "It's just up the road from our place. It's a dead end, and his place is the two-story with the big window upstairs. I'm sure you'll see his roadster in the driveway, and his name is on the mailbox out front. Just set your GPS and let it take you there."

On the drive from Boulder, Paula thought carefully about what she would say to Boyd, how she would explain her indefensible behavior and the unreasonable charges she had laid at his feet. Nothing she could say would justify what she had done, and she knew that he had given up on her. He no longer made any attempt to contact her, and the onus was on her. She had to convince him to forgive her.

It was dusk when she arrived and was relieved to see his car, and no other, in the drive. Hopefully she had caught him alone. There was a low light in one room, but the other rooms were dark. "Please don't let him have a woman with him."

She wrapped herself in the comfort of her son's words and mounted the steps to the front door. She lifted the heavy brass knocker and rapped three times, then held her breath until the door opened.

He was unshaven and looked tired, but Paula's

heart leaped when she saw him looking like everything she wanted in the world. In that moment, she knew he was the fulfillment of every need, every wish, every desire in her life, and she shuddered to think she had tried to throw it all away.

A light flared in his eyes when he recognized her, but he quickly shuttered his gaze. "Paula." He stood very still, unreadable.

She waited for him to invite her in. When he failed to do so, she cleared her throat and clasped her hands in front of her. Her breath caught as she croaked, "May I come in?"

He shook his head as if to clear it. "Oh, sorry. Yes. Of course, come in." There was no warmth in his voice. He stepped back and waved her into the cabin. "Can I get you something? Coffee, a drink?"

She thought he appeared disturbed at her sudden appearance so far from Boulder. Did he think she had come to have him arrested? There was nothing in her manner to indicate her intentions. She shook her head. She had to get this over, even if it meant he would never forgive her. But just starting took a great leap.

"I don't know where to start. I went to your office, and Lottie said you had come up here. It's beautiful. No wonder you like to spend free time here."

He didn't respond. They waited, simply looking at each other. She started again, "And I didn't know how to reach you, so I called Helen King, and she gave me directions to get here."

"I see."

"So, here I am," she finished. Her words sounded stupid to her own ears.

She had known it would be hard, but found herself tongue-tied. Her legs shook, but she took a deep breath and steadied her voice the best she could. "You were right about so many things, Boyd. I wanted to punish someone for Sam's death, even though I knew it wasn't your fault."

"That's right."

"I was lonely and angry and bitter, and I believed everything Sam said about you."

"I know."

"It would have been easier if there hadn't been this *thing* that sprang up between us the moment I met you. I had to fight a battle on two fronts—my battle against you for Sam and my battle against you for myself. It was exhausting."

He remained standing just inside the room. "I'm sure."

"When we made love..." Her voice faltered, but she hard and continued, "When we made love I felt a wash of guilt and confusion, and I blamed you for taking advantage of me." She looked at the floor. "It wasn't fair to you."

"No, it wasn't."

"I know that now. And I want to apologize. I tried to make you the villain. You weren't. It was my fault."

A silence fell. "You drove a long way to apologize. Is that why you were looking for me?"

She wanted him to take over, to welcome her, but clearly was not going to. It was going to be up to her. "No, that's not the only reason."

She squeezed her eyes shut for just a moment, then looked into his eyes from across the room. He wasn't helping; he forced her to make a clean breast of it. "I've been looking for you to tell you—to tell you I love you."

He still didn't move.

"And," she hurried on, "that I love you without reservation, as you are, without question, without explanation. This is Paula Wincott, single woman, who loves you. You said you made love to me because you loved me. I think I've loved you since that moment as well. Now I can be honest with both of us."

"What about Sam's lab notes?"

"I don't know who took them, but I know it wasn't you. I wanted to believe you took them because I didn't have any other defense against you."

"The lab is no longer viable. You understand that?"

Their eyes met and held. He was pushing her, but everything hinged on complete understanding.

"The truth is, I don't care anymore. All I care about right now is whether you accept my apology so I can live with myself."

He nodded his head slowly and looked at her steadily. "Yes, I accept your apology. I never thought I'd hear it, and I know how much it cost you to offer it. We've been over a lot of rocky ground, and some ugly things have been said, but certainly I accept your apology."

They stood looking at each other. Was the elephant still sitting in the living room, blocking their way to each other? Did they still not trust each other?

After a long moment, she said, "Well, I guess that's it. I just wanted to let you know how I feel, how sorry I am that I behaved so badly, how much I regret. And how much I love you."

Holding her breath, she waited. He didn't move.

She turned toward the door. "Please say something so I don't have to go," she whispered, her voice barely audible. "I don't want to go." In a long and painful silence, she grasped the door handle and pulled it open.

As she started through the door, he murmured, "Wait. I don't want you to go. I don't *ever* want you to go."

She turned around to face him. He opened his arms to her.

"I love you, Paula Wincott. I will always love you. More than you can even imagine. Please, please stay with me."

Boyd crossed the room. In an instant she was in his arms, crushed against his chest. He held her urgently, without tenderness. "Foolish woman. Of course I love you. I can't tell you how much I love you. I thought I'd lost you forever."

He held her head firmly in one hand and sprinkled hot kisses all over her face. "I haven't liked you very much these past few weeks, but I do most certainly love you. I gave up that you would ever want me."

Her fingers were already at work on his belt, but she was shaking so hard she couldn't get the buckle undone. Desire rushed upwards from the point where his body had pressed against hers and she had felt his blatant erection. She groaned at the sheer pleasure of the sensation. He captured her lips with his and sucked her groan into his mouth where it blended with his ragged breath. He slipped his tongue between her open teeth and rubbed the inside of her mouth until her tongue answered his demand and met him with equal fervor, darting and returning, inviting and taunting.

****

He tried to move slowly, to be gentle, but it had been too long since they last made love, and he wanted her too much. Why was it always like this with her? Why did he lose himself so completely in her?

This time he would do it right. He scooped her up in his arms and carried her to his bed. His bed, not Sam Wincott's bed. If he had his way, she would never sleep in Sam's bed again. He deposited her gently and fell to the mattress with her. He tried not to tear her clothes from her body, holding himself in check while she tugged his jeans and shirt from him and ran her tongue over his belly, down, down, to that part of him desperate to enter her.

They undressed each other, and when she lay back and opened her thighs in silent invitation, he rubbed the hot tip of his penis against her for a moment, watching her face, then slid himself smoothly, until he was settled deep inside her. They made slow, beautiful love, punctuated with repeated declarations of mutual passion. When the white-hot flames at last had been quenched, they lay in each other's arms, limbs entangled, her head against his chest.

She nuzzled her head against him. "I can feel your heart beating against my cheek," she whispered, as if she had never heard a heartbeat before.

He kissed the top of her head and caressed her breast. "My heart beats only for you, my love."

She laughed softly, smothering the sound against his chest.

He lifted her chin and demanded, "Did that sound too corny?"

"Not at all," she said between giggles. "Well, yes, but I love to hear it. Tell me more corny love words. I'll never get tired of hearing them."

"I'll never get tired of saying them," he promised. "But the most important thing I can say to you right now is that you are never leaving me again. You'll sleep in my bed every night, and we'll wake together every morning, and people will say 'There goes that silly Paula Mackenzie who's always smiling.' But only you and I will know why you wake up smiling every morning."

She stroked the hair on his forearm and tilted her head to look up at him. "Paula Mackenzie? Are you asking me to marry you?"

"Of course. That's where this relationship was always headed. Didn't you know?" He backtracked a bit, "But you don't have to take my name if you don't want to. I'm a modern man, and you're not my possession. I just want you to be my wife. Please."

He looked so earnest that she hugged him tightly and rubbed her body against his. "Whenever you say, Professor."

Emma would have to learn to live with it. With the decision made, Paula felt a sense of liberation that was unimaginable. She laid her head against his chest and savored the joy that welled up in her heart.

****

She didn't go home that night, nor the next morning, nor the next. He tried to persuade her to move in with him, but she argued that she had years of living in her house that had to be gathered up and put away before they could get married. And she had to speak to Emma and Wesley in familiar surroundings. The truth about Sam was going to be difficult to explain to Emma without destroying the myth of her father, and Paula wanted to protect her from that.

After a few days of isolated bliss in his mountain hideaway, they returned to Boulder to make plans for their life together. She found a message on her answering machine from Wesley that partially lifted a burden from her heart.

"Hey, Paula, it's Wes. We got your message about Mackenzie, and, I must say it hit Emma hard. But she's not a fool, and she'll come to recognize that you're not either. Joe Peterson had already told me that there was no evidence whatsoever that Mackenzie had anything to do with Sam's lost papers. He said he had been on a fishing expedition and had turned up nothing. And everyone he spoke to had nothing but praise for this guy. Did you know he supported Sam's lab with money from his own funds? Joe knows somebody who knows somebody who's on

215

the inside, so it comes from a reliable source."

She sat down to absorb this message from Heaven. It wasn't going to be difficult after all.

"*So,*" Wesley continued, "*it seems he's a stand-up kind of guy. And that set me to wondering about Sam's attitude toward him. You know, all of those stories he used to tell us about how Mackenzie was out to get him. Then he blamed Mackenzie for the fact that he was forced to retire. Something didn't fit. I know my theory may upset you, as well as Emma, but I think Sam may have been suffering from... well, you know, paranoia. We'll talk later. I love you.*"

Paula couldn't have been more startled. Wesley had come to the correct conclusion all on his own, a conclusion that should have been apparent to everyone, most especially his family. But they had been blinded by the love and admiration they felt for the man who had guided all of them in all the decisions of the lives, the man on whose judgment they had always relied.

She turned off the machine and sat, assimilating the gist of his message. Wonderful Wesley. She was so grateful to him for his eternal optimism, his dedication to family, and his recognition of truth when it poked him in the eye.

CHAPTER TWENTY-SIX

Lottie's special day dawned on a typical Boulder spring morning, graced with sunshine, clean air, and millions of flowers blooming all over the hillsides. James and Lottie made a handsome couple. She a few pounds lighter in her ivory silk dress; he, a stocky Irishman in a perfectly-cut morning coat, beaming with happiness. Paula wept copious tears as the couple made their pledges to each other in the midst of the friends and well-wishers who had turned out for this special day. They had written their own vows and had even written certain portions of the ceremony for the officiating minister.

"I, James, take thee, Charlotte, as my eternal love and my wedded wife, and I promise to do everything in my power to make sure you never regret one millisecond of our life together. We are as two diamonds spinning in a silver spoon, catching each other's light and reflecting it back, ever brighter."

"I, Charlotte, take thee James, as my eternal love and my wedded husband, and I promise to honor and cherish you to the end of my life."

At the end of the ceremony, Jamie gently lifted Lottie's gauzy veil and landed a lusty kiss on her lips to the cheers and applause of the wedding party. The ceremony was held outdoors in a beautiful park setting, and cars of passersby honked their horns in support of the newlyweds. As a member of the wedding party, Paula stood beside Lottie in the formal photos, but Lottie insisted that Boyd stand on the other side of Paula, acknowledging his significance in her life.

When Lottie prepared to toss her bouquet, she lined herself up directly in front of Paula and threw it smartly into her arms. Then she angled her head toward Boyd and offered a wink broad enough to bring a bright blush to Paula's face. The wedding party applauded, and Paula blew her a kiss, accepting the import of the wedding bouquet.

"She's very astute lady," Boyd said with a grin. "But then I think everyone knows how I feel about you. As someone once said to me, it's as if I have a neon sign hung around my neck."

"I guess we both do," Paula conceded. "Everyone's been asking me when we're getting married, and I haven't even told anyone we're seeing each other. Are we that obvious?"

He leaned down to kiss her cheek. "Yes, my darling. We are. Why don't we just set the date and put everyone's questions to rest?"

While the photographer finished taking the last of the wedding photographs, the caterers had already begun setting up, and the orchestra was assembling. Boyd and Paula found their seats and made the acquaintance of their table-mates, a few of James's friends and a few of Lottie's, all warm and charming.

"How have you and your husband known Lottie and James?" asked a sweet-faced brunette at Paula's elbow.

She started to answer that Boyd wasn't her husband, but he leaped ahead of her and answered cordially. "Lottie's been a member of our department ever since I can remember." He turned to Paula. "Isn't that right, darling?"

"That's right," she agreed. "And she's been a friend for all of those years as well."

"So, you're part of the Chemistry department at the university?" queried an angular blonde in a large picture hat. "Did you know that Hastings woman?"

The brunette looked around then leaned in close. "Was that her name? You're talking about the one who was caught stealing and had to be dismissed? I thought her name was Billings, wasn't it?"

Paula's skin prickled. Billings? Wasn't there an Amy Billings in Sam's lab?

The blonde nodded, taking in the whole table. "Yes, that's it—Billings. I heard from Carol Oakes that she destroyed some valuable lab notes but wasn't prosecuted because she's a little off her rocker, if you know what I mean."

She twirled her finger at the side of her temple to demonstrate. "It was handled very discreetly," she continued knowingly, "and it never made the newspapers. Carol heard it from her son's girlfriend who goes to CU."

Wide-eyed, the brunette asked Boyd, "So, did you know her? The Billings woman?"

His face remained impassive. "I don't think I recognize the name. There was no one by that name in my area of biochemistry."

He lifted a bottle of champagne from the ice bucket and asked, "Is everyone ready to toast the bride and groom?"

So that was it. Amy Billings, the brightest of Sam's graduate students. Now Paula knew the truth. But it wasn't important.

She knew it wasn't Boyd, and that was all that mattered. She had never been more proud of another human in her life as she was of him at this moment. He had refused to stoop to gossip and had never offered any information about that poor girl's part in the theft.

Her heart swelled with the depth of love she felt for this man. It frightened her to think that her own blind prejudice might have denied her the joy she

219

had found in his arms.

When he poured the champagne into her glass, she reached under the table to caress his thigh while she looked into his eyes and promised, "How about a June wedding, Professor?"

Her hand slid into his lap and felt his flesh quicken beneath her touch. His hand shook only slightly as he raised his glass. "I'll drink to that."

A word about the author...

Sharon Noble lives with her husband and two dogs in Los Angeles, where she teaches English grammar and Accent Reduction at the Beverly Hills Lingual Institute. She is also a working actor, and her TV/film credits can be found at IMDB, the Internet Movie Database.

She finished her Master's Degree in Communications at the University of Colorado in Boulder, so it was a familiar and fondly remembered environment for her first romance, *Autumn Desire*.

She also has a particular affection for Winnipeg, Manitoba, where she taught Theatre Arts at the University of Winnipeg before moving to Los Angeles.

Sharon enjoys oil painting, tango dancing, and an occasional yoga class to offset the sedentary life of a writer.

She welcomes reader comments at her website
www.sharon-noble.com.

9 781601 547606